By the same author

Joy School

The Pull of the Moon

Range of Motion

Talk Before Sleep

Durable Goods

Until the Real Thing Comes Along

Until the Real Thing Comes Along

a novel

ELIZABETH BERG

Random House New York

Until the Real Thing Comes Along is a work of fiction. Names, characters, places, and incidents are the product of the author's imagination or are used fictitiously. Any resemblance to actual events, locales, or persons, living or dead, is entirely coincidental.

 Published in the United States by Random House, Inc., New York, and simultaneously in Canada by Random House of Canada Limited, Toronto.

Library of Congress Cataloging-in-Publication Data
Berg, Elizabeth.
Until the real thing comes along / by Elizabeth Berg.
p. cm.
ISBN 0-679-45722-4
I. Title.
PS3552.E6996S48 1998
813'.54—dc21 97-25206

Random House website address:www.atrandom.com
Printed in the United States of America on acid-free paper
24689753
First Edition

Book design by Lilly Langotsky

For Julia Marin

and

Jennifer Sarene

and in memory of

James Allen Gagner

Acknowledgments

My editor, Kate Medina, and my agent, Lisa Bankoff, have been with me from the start, and I am grateful.

Thanks to Jessica Treadway, who read this book in manuscript with special intelligence and sensitivity.

And deepest thanks—as always—to Jean-Isabel McNutt, whose skill and perseverance I so admire.

Until the Real Thing Comes Along

Prologue

This is how you play the house game:

Go for a drive to somewhere you've never been. At the point when the spirit moves you, start looking for your house. You can choose whatever you want, at any time; and once you choose it, it is yours. One caveat: after you've made a selection, you can't change your mind. If you pick the white colonial with the pristine picket fence and then in the next block you see an even better colonial, it's too late; you must stay with your first choice.

I started playing this game as a little girl, and I still play it. And I always pick too early, so it almost always happens that a much grander choice comes along. I might be expected to feel regret at such a moment, but I never do. I can admit to the superiority of another house; I can admire it and see every way in which it is better than my first choice, but I am never sorry. I know a lot of people have a hard time believing this, but it's true. I know a lot of people think it's an odd characteristic, too, but I have to say it is something I like about myself. It is, in fact, what I like most.

1

I used to think that the best thing to do when you had the blues was to soak in a bathtub full of hot water, submerge yourself so that only the top half of your head was in the outer world. You could feel altered and protected. Weightless. You could feel mysterious, like a crocodile, who is bound up with the wisdom of the natural world and does not concern herself with the number of dates she has per month or the biological time clock. You could feel purified by the rising steam. Best of all, you could press a washrag across your chest, and it would feel like the hand of your mother when you were little and suffering from a cold, and she'd lay her flat palm on you to draw the sickness out.

The problem with the bathtub method is that you have to keep fooling with the faucet to keep the water temperature right, and that breaks the healing spell. Besides that, as soon as you get out of the tub the solace disappears as quickly as the water, and you are left with only your annoying lobster self, staring blankly into the mirror.

These days I believe that museums are the place to go to lose your sorrow. Fine-art museums with high ceilings and severe little boxes mounted on the wall to measure the level of humidity; rooms of furniture displayed so truly the people seem to have just stepped out for a minute; glass cases full of ancient pottery in the muted colors of old earth. There are mummies, wearing the ultimate in long-lasting eyeliner; old canvases that were held between the hands of Vermeer; new canvases with emphatic smears of paint. The cafés have pastry as artful as anything else in the building; gift shops are stocked with jewelry modeled after the kind worn by Renaissance women—the garnet-and-drop-pearl variety. I buy that kind of jewelry, in love with its romantic history and the sight of it against the black velvet. Then I bring it home and never wear it because it looks stupid with everything I have. But it is good to own anyway, for the pleasure of laying it on the bedspread and then sitting beside it, touching it.

What I like most about museums is that the efforts of so many people remain so long after they are gone. They made their marks. If you are an artist, you can hope to achieve that. If you are not an artist, you believe that having children is the closest you'll come.

Well, that's what I believe. And anyway, I have always preferred the company of children; I just like to be around them. Whenever my large family gets together on holidays, I sit at the kids' card table. It's so much more relaxing, what with the way the dishes are plastic, and manners of any kind optional. So much more interesting, too—no talk about current events, no holding forth by any overweight, overeducated aunt or uncle. There is talk only about things that are astonishing. Facts about the red ant, say, or the elaborate retelling of an unfortunate incident, such as the one where a kid vomited on the teacher's desk.

I always thought I'd have five or six children, and I have imagined so many lovely domestic scenes featuring me and my offspring. Here we are outside on a hot summer day, running through the sprinkler. The children wear bright fluorescent bathing suits in pink and green and yellow; I wear cutoffs and a T-shirt. There is fruit salad in the refrigerator. Later, I will let the older kids squirt whipped cream for the younger ones; then, if they pester me enough in the right way, I'll let them squirt it into their mouths—and mine.

Or here I am at the grocery store, my married hands unloading graham crackers and packages of American cheese that have already been broken into due to the eager appetite of the toddler in the carriage, who is dressed in tiny OshKosh overalls over a striped shirt. His fine hair, infused with gold and red, curls up slightly at the back of his neck. His swinging feet are chubby and bare; he has flung his sneakers and socks on top of the family-size pack of chicken breasts. His brothers and sisters are in school. Later in the afternoon, he will stand at the living-room window, watching for them to come home, squealing and bending his knees in a little joy dance when he sees them marching down the sidewalk toward him, swinging their lunch boxes in high, bright-colored arcs.

I have imagined myself making dinner while my dark-haired daughter sits at the kitchen table. She is making me a picture of a house with window boxes, choosing crayons with slow care. She is wearing yellow turtle barrettes in her hair, and a bracelet she made from string. "Hey, Mommy," she says, "do you want flowers on the ground, too?" Oh yes, I say. Sure. "Me too," she says. We smile.

I have imagined a fleshy constellation of small children and me, spread out and napping on my big bed while the newest baby sleeps in her crib. The pulled-down shades lift with the occasional breeze, then slap gently back against the windowsill. If you listen carefully, you can hear the small breathing sounds of the children, their soothing, syncopated rhythms. There is no other sound, not even from the birds; the afternoon is holding its finger to its lips. All the children have blankets and all of them are sucking their thumbs. All of them are read to every night after their baths. All of them think they are the favorite. None of them has ever had an illness of any kind, or ever will. (I mean, as long as I'm imagining.)

What I never imagined was the truth: me at thirty-six years of age, lying around on top of my made bed on a beautiful winter afternoon with shades pulled for an entirely different reason, thinking, Why didn't I marry Johnny Tranchilla? So he was shorter than I was. He was very handsome and very romantic. He had black curly hair and naturally red lips. He sent me a love note in the mail after our first date and he was only nineteen, how brave! His father was loaded. He wore Weejuns with no socks. I could have been happy. Then I go on through the rest of my short list, thinking of the men I might possibly have married. Ron Anderson, who became a mildly famous artist and now lives in a huge A-frame in the Rocky Mountains with his blonde wife, who is more beautiful than I'll ever be but not as much fun, I can guarantee it. She would never have broken into the planetarium like I did with Ron, would never have entered into the famous mustard-and-catsup fight at D.J.'s diner at three in the morning.

There was Tim Connor, too, who was quiet and tender and reliable—not exciting, but one grows tired of that after one is, oh, say, ninety-five. Frank Olds became a neurosurgeon! I could have lived in material comfort instead of making dinners out of soda crackers and cottage cheese and repeatedly showing houses to people who will never buy any of them.

The reason I didn't marry any of the various men I might have is always the same: Ethan Allen Gaines. I fell in love with him in sixth grade, and I never, never stopped loving him, not even after we tried to have a serious relationship in our late twenties and failed, and he took me out to dinner to a very nice place to break off our engagement and told me it was because he was gay. "Oh, Ethan," I said, "that's okay, I'll marry you anyway." It was as inadvertent and embarrassing as a piece of meat flying out of my mouth. Ethan nodded, looked away. And then back at me. And I knew that was the end of that. Knew it in my head, anyway. The heart is always a different matter. I kept the ring. It lives in a box as beautiful as it is.

"I told you," my friend Elaine said the day after we broke up. "I *told* you! Who else would keep rolled-up towels on their bathroom sink?"

"They were *hand* towels," I said.

". . . And?"

"A lot of people roll up their hand towels."

"Patty. It wasn't just the towels."

"*I* know," I said. "I know!"

But I hadn't known. I hadn't let myself.

Because consider this: once Ethan and I were at a lake and he rented a boat because I said I had never learned how to row. He told me what to do, made me get in alone, and watched from shore, shouting encouragement. I got stuck. I dropped an oar. Ethan was telling me how to come in with one oar, but I was just going around in circles. "I can't do it!" I yelled. He put a hand to his forehead, shielding his eyes, and yelled back, "Yes, you can!" But I couldn't. And so he waded out to me in his beautiful new brown tweed pants and white sweater and pulled me in. And I sat, hanging onto both sides of the boat, watching the sun in his yellow hair and the moving muscles of his back. And when he got me in, we sat in the grass and he was wringing out his pants and sweater and dumping water from his shoes and I said I was so sorry, I knew how expensive those clothes were—they were from Anthony's, a very exclusive men's shop that served you Chivas in a cut-crystal glass while you fingered linens and silks. Ethan asked if I wanted to go shopping and I said sure, I'll buy you some new clothes, but not from Anthony's. He said no, I'll buy an outfit for both of us. I said, I ruined your pants! Why would you buy me an outfit? And he said because you can't row a boat.

The day before that, we'd been to see a movie with an exquisitely sad ending, the kind that makes your insides feel made of glass. My throat ached when the lights came up; I wanted to just run out of there so I wouldn't have to hear anything anyone said. Ethan's face seemed full of what I felt, too. "Run," he whispered, and we did. We ran to his car and slammed the doors and sat still, staring straight ahead and saying not one word. Then I looked over at him and he took my hand and said, "I know."

On the night Ethan told me he was gay, I said that admitting it must be a very liberating experience, that it must feel good. He said it did in many ways, but it hurt him that he had to hurt me. I said, well, we would always be best friends, wouldn't we? He said of course.

I didn't cry until I came home and climbed into the bathtub. Then I sobbed for a good twenty minutes. And then I leaned back, laid the washrag over my chest, inhaled the steamy air, and thought about when Ethan had come over when I was sick, just a few weeks earlier. He'd made chicken soup and three kinds of Jell-O, brought with him a variety of cheeses and crackers and fruit. He'd treated me with a tenderness that was somehow too competent. I'd watched him, longing for him to come over to me, kneel down, knock over my ginger ale, ignore it, take my hand, and say, "If you ever die, I'll kill myself." But he didn't do that. He ran his hand sweetly over my forehead, went to adjust the flame under the soup; then, frowning, flipped through the channels on the television. He covered me with a quilt he'd laundered, patted my feet affectionately, then made a phone call. I felt as though he were zipped into a self that was hiding the real him—I could get close, but not *there.* I had put it down to a normal kind of male reticence, the kind that has a woman sigh and put her hand on her hip and call a girlfriend. I had believed that with the trust and intimacy of marriage it would get better—he would open himself completely to me.

But that night, with my engagement ring newly off my finger (though the stubborn indentation of it remained), I slid deeper into the water and thought about all the times Ethan and I had made love. Then I thought about those times again, and saw them true. I pulled the washrag up over my face. Beneath it, I think I was blushing.

2

I have always thought that part of my problem is my name: Patty. That's what my parents named me. Not Patricia. Patty. Patty Anne Murphy. Sounds like one of those huge dolls that walk like Frankenstein's monster. Sounds like a huge, Irish-Catholic, curly-headed doll, not a desirable woman whom you want to marry and impregnate.

I don't know what my parents were thinking. Well, yes I do. I asked them recently, and they said they were thinking it was a clean and healthy name, a fun name.

Fun? I said.

Yes, they said, and then both of them started getting that hurt look that makes you feel like you're beating a puppy.

"You *can* change it," my mother said, sniffing, and I said no, no, I liked it, really, I was just wondering how they chose it.

"Why?" my mother said, happily suspicious. "Do you need names?"

Ma, I said, and she said all right.

She doesn't care if I'm married or not. Not anymore. She's

crazy about children, too. She understands the overwhelming want I have. She thinks the hell with a husband, if I can't find one—just have a baby. She'll help me, my brother and sisters will help me—they'll give me a million hand-me-downs. Probably Elaine could even pitch in on the weekends, she said, the last time she got going on this. Elaine could do a little baby-sitting on the weekends so I could go out and show houses, couldn't she? Might do *her* some good. My mother is mystified as to why neither Elaine nor I have married and had children. I don't exactly have a lot to pick from. Elaine's problem is that she has too much to pick from. My mother also told me about those services they have now, Parents in a Pinch, had I heard of them?

"Ma!" I said, finally. She smiled primly, then rose from the dinner table to clear the dishes, pointedly refusing my help. A dubious punishment, in keeping with her usual methods. Both of my parents were always terrible at punishing; if, for example, you were sent to your room, one or the other of them would inevitably join you up there.

People say, Wow, your mother's pretty liberal. But they're missing the point. The point is, she makes me feel so much worse. At work, when I'm supposed to be doing comp sheets, I sit at my desk, my hand over my uterus, thinking about how I have so few good eggs left. I imagine my inventory: rotten eggs, eggs empty of insides, misshapen eggs, all tumbling down my weepy fallopian tubes. And every now and then a really good egg, perfumed and made-up and beribboned, calling out, "I'm *ready*!", her little voice echoing in the vast darkness. "Yoo-hoo!" she calls, to no one. My uterus drums its fingers, yawns, wonders whether it should close up shop early, what's the point.

I once went to a bookstore to see if I could find something on keeping my eggs healthy. I didn't see anything, so I went over to customer assistance. I waited in the longer line, so I could have the woman, and then I said, very quietly, "Would you have anything on . . . you know, keeping your eggs healthy?"

"KEEPING YOUR *EGGS* HEALTHY????" the woman asked.

I blushed, nodded.

"This would be a COOKBOOK, right?" she asked, and started punching keys on her computer. She looked up at me over her half glasses, her spiky earrings swinging.

"Um . . ." I said. "Sure." And then I stood there and waited until she told me why yes, they had a book called *Safe Food* that would probably be exactly what I needed. Thanks, I said. And actually went to the shelf she pointed to. Actually looked through *Safe Food,* which had many frightening graphs and statistics and boldfaced definitions of digestive ailments. I looked through it for what I thought was a respectful length of time and then I put it back on the shelf. I felt like I needed to wash my hands. And then I felt bad for not buying the book, because the woman had gone to the trouble of looking it up.

This is how I am. It's really bad in small stores. If I go into one, I have to buy something. Otherwise I worry about hurting the feelings of the people who are working there. "You're so crazy, what do you *think*?" Elaine always says, when I buy useless items that I often donate to the Salvation Army without taking them out of the bag. "You think everyone who comes in that store buys something? You're *allowed* to just *look.*"

"*I* know," I say. "I just look, sometimes." But not in small stores.

This misguided tenderness of heart may account for my dismal record at work. My low number of sales. I have been at Rodman Real Estate for two years and I have sold one house. Which I did the first week I was there. It was a $3.2 million house and I just happened to answer the phone at the right time. The buyers had always admired the house and the moment it came on the market, they snapped it up. They told me how to do everything; they'd bought and sold a lot of houses. They were so *rich*! I wonder sometimes when people are that rich if they get annoyed that they can only get so good a brand of toilet paper, a kind anyone can have. You know, there they are in their luxuriously appointed bathroom, with the gold fixtures and the Italian marble floor, and all they can put on their $700 dispenser is quilted Northern.

I am currently living off the last bit of my profit from that sale, and waiting for the next fluke. It has to happen soon or I'll have to find another job, which I really don't want to do. Because even though I am lousy at it, I love the real estate business. I like helping people find a home where they think they'll be happy. And I like seeing how other people live, imagining myself frying eggs in this country kitchen, watching television in that blue-carpeted family room. Here I am in the English garden that you get to through white French doors; there I am in my library, the walls lined with oak paneling, the leaded-glass windows reaching from floor to ceiling. Or, my favorite: Here I am in a little bedroom in my little cottage that is right on the water. I am in my baby's room, rocking her, listening to the rush and pull of the waves outside the window, and singing a made-up song into an ear more shell-like than shells. My baby's fist holds tightly onto my finger, even as she fades into sleep. I look at the faint scribble of vein across her tiny eyelid. I pick up her foot, examine her littlest toe, softly exclaim my delight.

Always back to the same place, lately.

It's an obsession, I'll be the first to admit that.

Anyway, in real life, most of my showings are to the Berkenheimers, who are looking for a vacation home. Crystal Cove, Massachusetts, where I live, has an interesting mix of small cottages and huge mansions, and everyone seems to get along. Upscale restaurants and those that serve dinner specials for $3.99 exist side by side; the cooks smoke and chat outside their backdoors. You can shop at Theresa's, where the elegance of the decor makes customers speak in hushed tones (and you can pay $140 for a cotton summer dress); or you can shop in the basement at Winkle's—that's where they have their women's department, in the basement. There are no changing rooms—you take it all off in the aisles and inspect yourself in mirrors that are hung on support columns and filmed over yellowly with time. There isn't a woman alive who wouldn't appreciate a mirror like that on certain days, if not, in fact, on most days. NO MEN! the big sign hanging above the stairs down to the basement reads. Because of that sign—held up, I happen to know, with dental floss—you don't have to worry about some guy seeing your torn underwear, or your belly in the not-held-in position. It's like a locker room for women of all ages—without the worry of an upcoming game. I like to hang out there even when I don't need clothes. I like to hear the support that women give each other, biting their lips and telling the truth about whether back fat shows in a bathing suit. ("Just tuck it in," I once heard a woman tell her friend. "And then

hold it down with duct tape. That's what they do on *Miss America*."
"Is duct tape waterproof?" her friend asked, and the room stilled to listen to the answer.)

About half of us live here in Crystal Cove year-round, and we practically congratulate each other when we pass on winter-deserted streets. The rest pull in for Memorial Day, leave after Labor Day. Their pretty houses sit empty the rest of the time, alarm console lights glowing day and night, although most theft around here has to do with skateboards.

The Berkenheimers live in a suburb north of Boston and their apparent vocation is driving here a few times a month and looking at every low-cost piece of property on the market, many of which they have already seen. Once Muriel, the wife, asked to see one of the most expensive mansions. Artie, her husband, started yelling at her.

"It's just for *fun,* Artie," she said. "Which you have forgotten how to have. About forty years ago, you forgot."

"About forty years ago I had something to have fun with," he said.

She took off her gigantic black sunglasses, turned around and stared at him sitting in the backseat of my car, sweating a little. He always has to sit in the back because if Muriel sits there, she gets nauseated. "Excuse me," she said. "Have you had a good look in the mirror lately? You want to know from forty years ago?"

"*Did* you want to see the place on Deer Run?" I asked my windshield.

"She's crazy," Artie said, waving his hand. "Mrs. Nutty Fruitcake."

"I'll show it to you," I said.

"Well, of course we can't afford it," Muriel said, her voice low. She pulled a handkerchief out of her purse, dabbed at her nose with it, stuffed it back in her purse. I saw a banana in there, dangerously ripe, and half a bagel, entombed in plastic wrap.

"I know you can't afford it," I said. "I don't mind. It'll be fun."

"We should maybe wash first," Artie said.

There was a moment of silence. Then Muriel said, "Oy, you hear this? '*We,*' he says. Like I've got a problem. Have I got a problem? I don't have a problem."

This is the way it goes with them. But they always treat me to lunch in a nice place because they feel so terrible about never buying anything. And their grandchildren are adorable and sometimes they'll bring one along. And then while they argue loudly in other people's kitchens, I take the little boy or girl outside to play. Sometimes there's a swing set. Sometimes we look for things on the beach. Sometimes we find something good—blue beach glass in a perfect oval shape, a shell with all the pinks of an A+ sunset, a crab scuttling away to safety.

It's not a terrible job. I mean, the Berkenheimers and I got to look at a beautiful house for a good forty minutes that day. The kitchen was roughly the size of a basketball court. There was a third-floor game room with a mahogany bar and a huge pool table, the requisite stained-glass lamp hanging low over the center. Artie and I took a few shots while Muriel inspected the bathrooms. She came up to the game room clutching her chest. "Solid marble," she whispered. "Pink! I swear to God." The closets were cedar; there were beautiful parquet floors; the swimming pool had a nice view of the ocean. You could be in the water looking at the water. We had a good time. We had a lot to talk about over lunch. And when I got back to the office, there was a message for me. A family of four, moving here for sure, needed a place within the next two or three weeks. "Even you can get a sale out of this," my boss Michael told me. Nicely—he really likes me. He's married.

But I didn't make that sale. Angela Ramsey did, she was working on the day they finally found a house, while I sat at home with the flu.

But the point is, there's always hope, you never know.

As in, the egg comes down the fallopian tube. The sperm leaps out with a box of candy. They get along. They really get along. Nine months later, I really am nursing a baby in the rocker—and soundlessly crying with relief. I tent the baby's head with her receiving blanket so the tears won't fall on her. And what color is her hair? Mine, exactly.

It hurts like a knife blade, this longing. If anyone knew how often I think about having a baby, I'd die of embarrassment. Which would take care of the problem, at least. But my plan is to not have it come to that. My plan is to get going right now in a very scientific and purposeful way that will lead to marriage and pregnancy. A husband and a child. The specifics of the plan I'm not too clear about. Only the intention.

3

On Saturday, I go to the library and look at the shelf that has books on relationships. There aren't many, but there's one called *Mr. Right? Right!* that seems promising. The jacket says this is a realistic approach to forming a relationship that is virtually guaranteed to lead to marriage. The author, a nonthreateningly attractive blonde woman, sits in a chair in what appears to be her office. There are many books on the shelf behind her, but you can't read any of the titles. I wish you could. I want to trust this woman. If I liked her books, we'd be off to a good start. I stare into her eyes: blue, friendly. Her jewelry is a simple gold wedding ring and a watch with a brown leather band. Pearl studs. She is wearing a white, long-sleeved blouse, open at the throat, blue jeans, and red cowgirl boots. At the end of her bio, it says she lives in New York City with her husband and infant daughter. Infant daughter, huh? I slam the book shut, go to the desk to check it out. Mary Ann, the fortyish librarian, leafs through it before she hands it back to me. "Let me know if it's any good," she says. I notice for the first time her ringless left hand. "All right," I say. We nod at each other.

We'll talk more later. I'll take her out for a cup of coffee. I'll say, "God, Mary Ann, are you miserable and desperate, too? I didn't know that! I'm so glad!" It's too busy to talk now; there are crooked lines of kids with crooked stacks of books pressed hard against their chests. You can tell the real book lovers; they stare silently ahead, reading the books in their minds already.

When I get home, I see Sophia, the neighbor who lives above my basement apartment, sitting out on the steps waiting for me. She has some mail in her lap, and I know why. She barely reads English, and what she does read she takes quite literally. Therefore junk mail gets her very excited. It's up to me to set her straight over and over again; she never believes her husband when he tells her it's all bullshit. Today is going to be exceptionally difficult—I see that the Publishers Clearinghouse envelope has arrived.

"I can be already winned," she tells me, before I've even reached her. She holds up the envelope. "Here is numbers."

I follow her into her apartment, sit at her kitchen table, sigh.

"This one is for true," she says over her shoulder, as she hangs up our coats.

"Sophia—"

"No! Some one body does win this!"

I stare into her pretty brown eyes. She must be at least seventy, but she still has a beautiful face. "That's right," I tell her. "Some *one* person does win this."

"So?"

"Fine," I say. "I'll help you. Did you pick out what car you want for the bonus prize?"

"There is car, too?"

"Yes." I find the insert, show her.

Her eyes tear. "I never forget you help me."

"Listen, Sophia, I just have to tell you, your chances are so, so slim. You understand? You do not have a good chance to win."

"I pick red one," she says. "Convergeable."

"Fine. Good. What else have you got there?"

She holds up another one of the letters. "Here, I can buy plate of kittens from famous artist." She shows me the color photo of the painted plate, blurrily displayed on a wooden holder. She shrugs, then muses in a high, soft, singsong voice, "I don't know, what you can do with some thing like this." She stares at the plate a little longer, then turns to me to ask, "Have you know of this artist?"

I shake my head.

She looks at the plate again, then puts the letter back in the envelope. "Okay. No thanks, I do tell them."

"You don't have to tell them. You can just throw it away. They only send it if you ask them to."

"Oh. Yes. I forget."

Next she shows me a white envelope with excited red print on the front. "This, I don't know what is it."

"It's for car insurance."

"I don't have car."

"I know. So just throw it away."

She puts the letter in her housecoat pocket. "When convergeable comes, I look on it again."

"Let's finish your entry, Sophia. I have to go make dinner. Ethan's coming over."

Sophia widens her eyes, clenches her fist, thumps at her chest with it. "*Beau*tiful," she says. "He is more than all what I seen in movie."

I feel an illegitimate surge of pride. "Do you really think so?"

She nods, adjusts the wide strap of her brassiere. "Give me some picture of him to dream on."

"I don't think I have any." Huh. I don't think I do.

"I take one his sock, then." She smiles, and the gold from her front tooth glints. "Is joke," she says seriously.

"I know."

Sophia never wears socks. She wears only orangeish-colored nylon stockings that she twists into knots below her knees. And then she wears Nikes with them, double-tied. She wears housecoats except on Sundays, when she wears severe dark suits and low heels and earrings that dangle just the tiniest bit.

Actually, I do have a pair of Ethan's socks. A gorgeous brown paisley weave. Once when I stepped in an icy puddle on the way to his house, he gave me a pair of his socks to change into. On days when the blues suck the life out of me and I never change from my bathrobe, I wear his socks to add a little class to the outfit.

"You always make so much!" Ethan says.

"You can take home leftovers," I tell him.

He sighs unhappily, eyeballing the huge pan of eggplant parmigiana that's sitting on the table between us, approximately one-twentieth of it gone.

My phone rings. I answer it, hoping it is some interesting man who has just realized how much he cares about me. Then I can turn to Ethan and say, "Just leave, since you're so ungrateful. Take your eggplant and get out of here. I'm busy."

"Yes, hello, Patty?" I hear.

"Yes?" Yay. Testosterone.

"This is Mark."

". . . Who?"

"Mark? Hansen?"

Silence.

"Uh . . ." he says. "Is Ethan there?"

There is not much that can deflate you more than your own phone ringing in your own house where you are the only one living there and then it's for someone else.

"Yes, one second," I say. I hand Ethan the phone, start clearing the table. I'll just be the maid. I'll just tidy up.

Ethan pulls the phone cord taut, talks in a low voice with his back to me.

I make loud kissing sounds, and the feel of my lips on my lips reminds me that it's been so long since I've been kissed by anyone but my family members. Ethan turns around to narrow his eyes at me and I shrug, fill the sink with soapy water.

He gets kissed all the time, Ethan. I'm sure of it. And he's such a good kisser. I remember. I love a good kisser. I love when your chest tightens and a whole rush of warmth moves down in you until you feel it in . . . Well. Here I am, rubbing a Brillo pad with a little too much energy over a fork that was clean long ago.

Ethan hangs up. Then he comes over and puts his arms around me from behind. We are the perfect image of a happily married couple, me wearing an apron and washing up the pretty plates, him pulling me close, his chin on my shoulder, his voice in my ear. Why does he have to be gay? It's just hostile.

"That was really for you," he says.

"What was?"

"The phone call."

I turn around, confused. "What do you mean? He asked for you!"

Ethan picks a plate out of the dish rack, starts drying it. "It was a guy I work with who wants to date you."

"What?"

"I told him about you. And I was supposed to tell you about him tonight. And then he was going to call, to make a date with you. He was asking if I'd told you yet. He's kind of eager."

"Well, forget it. You know how I feel about blind dates. I'm through with them. I'm never doing one again." *Eager.*

"You should do this one."

"It never works."

"Just do this one, and I promise I'll never ask you again."

"What's he like?" I say tiredly. And then while we finish the dishes, I listen to the usual careful superlatives.

I know one woman who still likes blind dates. I can't believe that she does, but she does. I am so sick of the drill: getting excited while you shave your legs in your new and too-expensive bubble bath, thinking no, but really, this one *could* be the one! You put on your makeup with extra care, you think about the cute stuff he said on the phone, you select your underwear with a certain mind-set. Not the first date, you're thinking, never on the first date, but hey, you never know, you might want to offer a sexy preview. You pace in your living room in your (new) heels before he arrives, see his car pull up, feel your hands start to sweat, hear the bell, open the door, smile brightly, and want the date to be over immediately. Because I don't care what people say, you can tell in three seconds if it's going to be good and I have yet to have a blind date where I opened the door and thought, Oh, wow, this is going to be good. No. What I always think is, Oh, God.

"Fine," I tell Ethan. "I'll go out with him."

We make our way to the sofa to see what's on TV and the phone rings again. I go over and pick it up. A man says, "Hi. This is Mark. Again."

"Yeah, okay, let's do it," I say.

"Pardon?"

"Let's go out."

"Oh! Okay. Tomorrow night? Dinner? I'll pick you up at seven-thirty?"

"That's fine," I say. At least I'll get a free meal. Assuming he pays.

I hang up the phone, sit down next to Ethan on the sofa, and burst into tears.

"Jesus," Ethan says. "What did he *say*?"

"I'm so *sick* of this," I blubber. "I just want to be done. I want to be married. I want a *ba*by."

"I know." He puts his arm around me.

"Why can't you love me?" I ask. "You love me, why can't you *love* me?"

"I . . ."

"You don't love anyone else."

"No."

"You want children, too."

"Yeah, I do. I really do."

"I read in a magazine that men's sperm counts are going down all over the world. And the sperm that *is* there isn't as healthy as it used to be. And let's face it, Ethan, you're not exactly getting any younger, either."

"I *know* that, Patty." Uh-oh. He's getting testy. Well, so am I.

"So why don't you just love me, goddamn it, Ethan! Or *don't*! I love you enough for the whole relationship. Just marry me and give me a baby! You can still see other men, I don't care."

I cannot believe I've said this. Is this what I really want? The room is very quiet.

I take in a deep breath, look into his eyes. "I mean, seriously, Ethan, how gay are you?"

He laughs, sadly. "Patty."

"Well, it's a continuum, isn't it?"

"I'm gay, Patty! I am attracted to other men! We've talked about this so many times. What can I say to make you understand that—"

"I *know*! But we could—"

"Don't," he says. "For God's sake."

I look away, talk to the wall. "See, I'm desperate. I've become desperate. I should be embarrassed right now, but I'm so desperate I'm not even embarrassed. Well. Maybe a little."

"You don't need to be embarrassed," Ethan says. "You just need to . . . move on. Listen, I think you'll really like Mark. *Really* like him."

I look down at my hands, which are gripping each other. I unclasp them, put them on my knees, try to relax. Then I look up at Ethan's beautiful face. At his blue eyes that can turn green. At the cheekbones a woman would kill for. He didn't shave today, and the sexy roughness on his face is enough to make me nauseated with desire. Sometimes I want to slap his face and say, Oh, just stop it! But of course you can't stop your looks.

You can't start your looks, either, not really. I ought to know. Check out my MasterCard bill for makeup. I'm not horrible, I can look okay. I'm just not anything like Ethan. I can't look so good it's dangerous. Men might on occasion turn their heads in a restaurant to watch me walk by, but they never stop chewing. They stop chewing for my friend Elaine. They stop *breathing* for my friend Elaine. Sometimes it's hard to be her friend. A lot it's hard to be her friend. I'm Betty to her Veronica, only I don't even get to have blonde hair.

It's not just Ethan's looks that I love. He makes me laugh all the time. He reads Shakespeare to me and makes it comprehensible; he taught me the thing about opera is that you have to breathe to it. When I order a second dessert, he won't say anything; often, he'll order a second one, too. He cries at sentimental commercials he's seen a hundred times. His wardrobe is beautiful, his manners so softly elegant. He is so tidy about losing his temper; I have never heard him yell.

"Ethan," I say, "I truly wish I didn't love only you, but that's the reality. I have loved only you since you saved me from Kathleen Mayfield on the playground in sixth grade." He was wearing a madras shirt that day, tucked into beautifully pleated pants. Little Weejuns. Kathleen was wearing a plaid dress with a bow at the neck which belied her personality. I remember seeing her skirt blow up over her head as she straddled me, pummeling me. She was angry because I'd laughed in gym class when the teacher said, "Now I am going to weigh you all. Is there anyone who has a problem with that?" Kathleen's voice boomed, "*I* do!" I laughed out of admiration, really; but Kathleen was not interested in any interpretation of the event but her own. So she was letting me know her opinion of me and Ethan came flying to the rescue. After a teacher broke up the scuffle, Ethan excused himself and went to the boys' room. He came out smelling of soap, with wet comb lines in his hair and with me smitten. "I have loved you since I discovered what love was," I say.

"I know, that's what you always say."

"It's true! I don't say it because it's cute, or romantic. It's a pain in the ass! But I feel like I'm the kind of person who finds one love in a lifetime. And you're the one."

He sighs, kisses my forehead.

Very, very slowly, I move my mouth toward his.

"Patty," he says gently, moving away. "Don't."

I am aware of the scent of his cologne now, rising up like a wall between us.

"Fine," I say.

I am all the time saying *fine* when what I want to do is hold the sides of my head and scream NO!!! I could get ulcers living this way. I bet I get ulcers. "Wow!" some cute married doctor will say. "Look how *many* you have!"

"I think I'd better go," Ethan says, rising, retucking his shirt into his pants, which hurts my throat.

"Ethan?"

"Yeah."

"Did you ever . . . how did you used to feel when we made love? How did that feel to you?"

He sighs, sits back down.

"It felt . . . it was very nice, Patty."

I nod.

"But . . . it was wrong. For me. There was something missing. It was painful, in that way."

"Okay."

"Can you understand?"

"But . . . You weren't telling the truth then, you were lying to me. Now that I know the truth, it would be different."

"Patty, what are you *asking* me?"

"I don't know. I don't know." I look at him. "To marry me?"

He opens his mouth and I say, "Oh, God. Never mind. I was, you know. I was kidding."

"I'll call you," he says, heading for the door.

"Ethan?"

"Yeah?"

"Could you just . . . would you try kissing me?"

He stands immobile.

"It's not like you've never done it!"

"I know. I know that."

"It would help me."

"No it wouldn't."

"Yes it would. You don't know what I mean, but I do." Actually, I don't know what I mean. I just want him to kiss me, and then kiss me again, and then everything will become very clear to both of us. Aha! he will say. I forgot! I *do* love you!

"Come on, just one time." I stand, take in a bumpy breath.

He sighs, comes toward me, lifts my chin with his pianist's fingers, lowers his face toward me. I raise my arms to encircle his neck, close my eyes.

There. There! Doesn't he feel how right this is? Doesn't he remember? I am so amazingly turned on. Isn't he? I open my eyes to steal a quick look at his face. I'm looking for the pretty anguish of passion. What I see is the resigned patience of, say, a nursing cow. Ethan's eyes are open, looking in the direction of the kitchen clock.

I step away, wipe my mouth with the back of my hand, though there is nothing to wipe away. "Just leave, you fuckhead," I say.

He closes the door quietly behind him. I'm still not embarrassed. Grief is taking up too much room.

I sit down at the kitchen table, use the serving spoon to start eating the eggplant we left out to cool. My stomach hurts from eating so much before, but I just keep on shoveling it in. I can see the headline: WOMAN, 36, CHILDLESS (NOT PREGNANT, EITHER), HOPELESSLY IN LOVE WITH GAY MAN, OVERDOSES ON LUKEWARM EGGPLANT PARMIGIANA. A lot of single women might hang the article up on their refrigerators, and every time they passed it they might shiver, thinking, *Wow, this could be me. Only I'd never be so stupid as to be in love with a gay man.*

I dial Ethan's number, listen to the message on his machine, say, "I'm sorry. Call me."

And then, I swear to God, I eat more eggplant.

4

The next morning, on my way to get a manicure (*not* because I have a date, I tell myself, though this is a lie), I stop for coffee at my favorite Dunkin' Donuts. There's a new guy behind the counter, young, maybe twenty, thin and anxious. His paper hat is bright white, ironed-looking. I order a large regular, milk, no sugar. He repeats the order back, then stands straight before me to ask, "Would you like to try one of our fresh hot bagels this morning?"

"No, thanks," I say. "Just the coffee." And then, "I'm sure another time I'll try one, though."

He hands me my coffee, makes change for my five-dollar bill.

"Sorry, I have to ask you that," he mumbles.

"That's okay."

He slides the cash-register drawer closed, looks around to see if the place is still empty. "They're not even really fresh," he says. "They're kind of hard."

"Oh. Well." I'm not sure whether I should offer thanks or sympathy.

I sit at a table by the window, look out at the deep blue sky. The clouds are thin, filmy; they look smeared on. Ethan left me a message while I was in the shower. He didn't call me last night because he got home too late. Uh-huh. Now he was on his way to the vet—his cat, Elton Jane, had not eaten in three days. Good, is what I say. I hate that cat. She's Himalayan, a puffed-out freak of nature, fluffiness gone to disgusting extremes, and she has a face that looks like it slammed into a wall. If you have to have a cat, get a little orange guy from the Humane Society, don't pay hundreds of dollars for some Greta Garbo feline who sits on top of the sofa staring slit-eyed at you, her contempt rising up off her like steam. She hates Ethan, too, so of course he loves her (you can see why I think there may be more heterosexual genes in Ethan than he's willing to admit). He actually serves her food in a cut-crystal glass, just like on TV. Imagine washing a Waterford glass with disgusting cat food stuck to the edges. He can't be gone for more than a few hours without worrying about her. He is just as ready for children as I am, Ethan. Well, he's not going to get them without a woman. It might as well be me.

I blow on my coffee, stare at a man coming in the door. What if he were my date for tonight? Hey! we'd both say. Didn't I see you this morning? The man looks at me, smiles. I smile back, straighten in my seat. Good-looking guy. Curly black hair. Dimples. Blue jeans, white T-shirt, flat stomach. I take a quick look at the black pick-up he got out of. O'Reilly Construction, it says on the side, in gold script. But maybe he's Mark Hansen, just working for O'Reilly. But Mark Hansen works at the same software company as Ethan; he doesn't do construction. Too bad. The door opens again, and a perky blonde dressed in workout clothes comes in. The man turns to her, asks if it was a large she wanted. "Uh-huh," she says musically, and slides up next to him. Where did she come from? His arm goes around her in a way that tells me they've slept together five thousand times. I turn away, look out the window again.

"Would you like to try one of our fresh hot bagels this morning?" I hear. The guy says, ". . . I don't know. Sure. Want one, hon?" The woman says, "No, that's okay. I'll just have a bite of yours."

Sometimes the feeling is that of a big steel door closing in my face. Well, obviously the guy is a moron, ordering a bagel in a doughnut shop.

A woman comes in pushing a stroller with a little boy, maybe eighteen months old, in it. He is holding a book upside down, studying the pages carefully. It is the puffy, waterproof variety of toddler book, perfect for bringing into the tubby. The woman turns the stroller so that the little boy faces me. He looks up from the book. I smile at him. He looks toward his mother, then back at me.

"Hi," I say softly.

He smiles slightly, kicks his feet up. They are wearing baby sneakers and baby socks. I feel my hand curling into a fist of longing. "Hi," I say again.

And now he smiles openly, revealing tiny white teeth. His mother, finished ordering (no thanks on the bagel, but how about one of them, uh, maple frostit coffee rolls), says, "Say HI, Daniel. Can you say HI?"

Daniel bites his book.

The woman smiles apologetically at me, but needn't. Everything about Daniel is perfect. I walk over, bend down beside him. "Hey," I say. I stroke his small hand. It's chubby, so soft, dimples lined up in a row at the knuckles. He regards me seriously, with the moist, new-looking eyes of the very young. I touch his cheek gently.

"Okay," the mother says, nervously turning the stroller around, away from me. "Let's see, Daniel, what kind of munchkin should we get you?"

I stand up, go back to my table full of shame. But I would never feed him munchkins, I'll tell you that. And I would use proper English around him.

"Aw," Amber says. "You didn't have to do this. Thanks!" She lifts the lid off the top of the coffee I've brought her. Her nails are gold today; maybe I'll try that. She sips cautiously through exceedingly red lips. Maybe I'll try that, too. In fact, maybe I'll go to school and become a manicurist. I like hanging around beauty shops. I like the smell of all the products, the sound of the hair dryers, the intimate chatter between client and hairdresser. What hairdressers hear would make therapists leap out of their chairs. Actually, maybe it's the therapists I hear talking to their hairdressers.

"What color today, babe?" Amber asks, inspecting my hands with a wrinkled brow. She takes her job seriously, and I am one of her tragic customers. "What happened here?" she asks sadly, pointing to a nail with a jagged edge.

I look at the nail with her. "I don't know."

She leans in closer. "Did you, like, use it to open something?"

I lean back, think a little. And then, "Oh! Yes! A CD!"

Amber leans back herself, sighs. "What have I told you?"

"I know."

"What? I want to hear it."

" 'Your fingernails are not a toolbox.' "

She nods, chews her gum seriously, gives me one of her oblique, I'll-give-you-one-more-chance looks.

"It was an emergency," I say.

"There are no emergencies that involve CDs." She starts removing my old polish, which was not a good choice: "Cancun Calypso" went with nothing but the outfit I was wearing that particular day.

"There are, too," I say.

She looks up. "Such as?"

"You could need to hear something right away."

"What, there's nothing in your house you can use to open a CD?"

"You might be in your car."

"You have a CD player in your *car*?"

"No."

"Your fingernails are not a toolbox," she says, not even bothering to look up.

"Fine."

"So what are you doing tonight?" She files my already short nails down farther. It tickles a little. I love getting manicures. I got my first one when I sold the house; it seemed like a ritzy treat. Now I do it about every two weeks. It makes me feel good. And I love Amber. She knows things.

I take a quick breath in, say quietly, "Blind date."

"Oy," she says, sympathetically. Everybody says "Oy" now.

Everybody says "Enjoy." Soon there will be one amalgamated culture and it will be so boring. There'll be no one to gossip about because everyone will be just like everyone else. However, I'll be dead by then.

"You know what percentage of blind dates turn into a serious relationship?" she asks.

I don't answer.

"Two point four."

"How do you know?"

"Read it."

"That's higher than I'd have guessed."

She snorts. "I had a blind date once, and the guy was a fucking undertaker."

"Oh, God. You didn't know?"

"No! He told me he was in public relations."

"So when did he tell you the truth?"

"When I wouldn't sleep with him."

"Oh. I see. Gee, funny it didn't work. Quite the aphrodisiac, being an undertaker."

"Yeah," she says. "What he called it was 'laying out stiffs.' I walked home from his house. Went flying out of there. Didn't have enough money for a cab."

I'll leave her a big tip. I feel a little responsible for her having to walk.

"So what color?" Amber asks.

"Oh! Uh . . . red?"

She raises her eyebrows.

"Just never mind," I say.

"You're kind of excited about this date, huh?"

"Please," I say. Meaning everything, I guess.

At two in the afternoon, I meet Ethan at the Tick-Tock Diner, our favorite. When one of the octogenarian regulars there complained about the café opening too late on the weekends (seven rather than six), Ed, the owner, gave him a key. Said he found him there the next morning making toast—had the coffee all brewed, too. It was kind of nice, Ed said.

"Now, let's *just* get something to *drink,*" Ethan said on the way in—we've both put on a few—but when the waitress came, he ordered a double bacon cheeseburger and banana cream pie.

"This is great," he says now, around his first bite. "Want some?"

"No. We're dieting, remember?"

Ethan looks at my sandwich, at the mile-high pile of stringy barbecued beef, the side order of cheese fries.

"I'm not going to eat all this," I say.

"Okay."

"I'm not!"

"So can I have a fry?"

"One."

"So," he says. "Are you excited?"

"I don't get excited about blind dates anymore. I get sick."

"You're not sick. You're excited."

I shrug, take another bite of sandwich, then smile at him. "Maybe."

Ethan picks a piece of meat off my sandwich, wedges it between his front teeth. "Hey, guess who I am?"

I sigh, inspect my teeth in the napkin holder, remove the offending morsel. "You know, you could have just quietly told me."

"I can't take you anywhere," he says, and uses his napkin to wipe a spot of sauce off my cheek.

"What if he doesn't like me?" I ask.

"He'll love you."

"How do you know?"

"I know him."

"What if I don't like him?"

"Now *there* will be something new. Why, you'll be able to knock me over with a feather!"

"What's that supposed to mean?"

"You never even try, Patty."

"Yes, I do!" No, I don't.

"Just try this time. For me."

"It wouldn't be for you."

"Yes, it would. I want you to find someone. One of us might as well."

"I thought you were seeing someone."

"Didn't work out. *I* have a blind date tonight, too."

"Oh, God."

"But I try. I really try."

"Do you?"

"Yes."

"Aren't you scared to?"

"I'm scared to death. For lots of reasons. But I do it anyway. You have to. Can I have more?"

I slide my plate to him, watch the way he picks up a fry, then chews it. I love everything about him, the way his leather jacket lies in the booth, the way he makes his capital *E*s, the way he eats. I look at my watch and wish it were hours later and I were sitting here with Ethan again, both of us done with what separates us.

Later, in the bathtub, I look through the Victoria's Secret catalogue. I want every hairdo I see. Plus every body. Even a few of the clothes. Which I won't get. I will dog-ear the pages, maybe even fill out the order form, but I won't get anything.

There was a message from Mark on my machine when I got home: dress very casually. So the guy's cheap.

I dress in jeans and a T-shirt, a white one, which I got on sale at Ann Taylor and which I think is pretty classy-looking, especially when I wear just my little gold earrings with it, no other jewelry except my watch, which I would not be caught dead without. I heard of a woman who wears two watches, in case one stops working. I understand completely. I must know what time it is, at all times. It's interesting to me. Plus I need a watch so I can tell the exact second tonight when it wouldn't be too rude to say, "Well, I do have to work tomorrow. . . ." One good thing about real estate is you can say that. You can say you have to work anytime—weekends, late nights, early mornings—because you do.

At 7:15, I'm ready. I lie down on my bed and close my eyes, take some deep breaths. If I weren't doing this, I'd have nothing to do tonight. I'd watch some movie, or read, or go to a mall and walk around aimlessly. I've heard you can meet men at those gigantic bookstores, but all I ever see there are married men. Or gay men. Or men who are going to qualify for Social Security in fifteen minutes. Actually, those are the kind of men I meet no matter where I go. So, fine. I have a date. Maybe I'll have some fun.

The doorbell rings. I startle, check my watch: 7:20. Could it be wrong? This makes me more anxious than the fact that my date is here. I check the clock by my bedside: 7:20, it says, and so does the one on my dresser.

I look out the window. In front of my house is a green Jeep, a few years old. Clean. Well, this tells me nothing. A Saab, I would know something. A pickup with a gun rack, I would know something. Or, you know, a Porsche. But a Jeep could be great or awful. I hate that.

The doorbell rings again. I run to the mirror, fluff up my hair, smile at myself, and then go to the door and open it. Because I have to.

"I'm sorry," he says. "I'm early, aren't I?"

"Well . . ." I say. Blue eyes, brown hair, a nice, shaggy cut. Not too fat and not too skinny. Jeans, a plaid shirt. Sleeves rolled up. A slight smell of some nice aftershave.

"Wait—you are Patty, right?"

"Yes," I say, and smile for real.

"Wow," he says. "You're pretty."

"Let me get my jacket," I say, and boy, do I step lightly to get it. Because for once in my life I am not thinking, Oh, God. Well, maybe I am. But in an entirely different way.

5

My mother has made lemonade for me, which I appreciate. She used real lemons, and served it in a tall, frosted tumbler with a jaunty sprig of mint. Now I am sitting at the kitchen table, watching her make marinade for the salmon she's serving for dinner.

"What's his name again?" she asks.

"Mark Hansen."

"Well . . ." she says, smiling. I know she wants to say more, but is afraid to. In her head, she is no doubt saying this: Patty Hansen. Patty Hansen. Not bad.

"I think I'm, you know, probably going to see him again," I say.

"I would think so." She runs water into a bowl, looks at me, then away.

"What?" I say.

"Nothing."

"What?"

"Nothing! Just . . . I've got a feeling, all right?"

"What feeling?"

"That this . . . It might . . . Never mind." She wipes her hands on the striped dishtowel, hangs it neatly over the edge of the sink. Then she comes to the table and sits down with me. "I just think this is a very unusual man you've met here."

"He's okay."

"You want to clean some carrots with me?"

"Sure."

She is a marvel in self-restraint. As am I. We are being so careful to avoid looking at each other I have a sudden fear that if we do, we might both ignite.

She divides up a pile of carrots, hands me one of the peelers. And then, when both of our heads are safely bowed over our work, she says, "I have to say, I really do like the idea of a nighttime picnic. The candles and all."

"And at his old Boy Scout camp!" I say.

"And running down that hill together, that was charming."

"He did that when he was a little boy."

"Yes, you said."

"Oh. Right."

I put down the peeler. "Mom. I don't know what this is."

She nods, reaches for my hand. "Maybe it's love, honey."

"It can't be, already."

She leans back, sighs. "Oh, yes it can. How do you think it happened to me and your father?"

"I don't think you ever told me."

"Didn't I?"

"No."

"Oh, my. Well, we met at a dance. He was in uniform. I know

what you think of uniforms, but I'm telling you, he was such a handsome sight. And it was instant, I swear to you. It just was. One look, and I was in love."

"Was he?"

"Well, I never asked him. But I think so."

"You never asked him?"

"No."

"Well, ask him!"

She smiles, and in it I see the nineteen-year-old she was when she met my father: the forties curls, the limp corsage on her padded-shoulder suit jacket.

"Ask him!"

She turns toward the den, yells, "Robert?"

No response.

Again, louder, she yells, "*Rob*ert?"

"WHAT?" he yells back.

"Did you fall in love with me at first sight?"

A moment. And now he is here, holding the newspaper, his glasses barely hanging on to the end of his nose, his hair sticking up a little in the back. I think he was sleeping. "What did you say?" he asks.

"Did you fall in love with me at first sight?"

"What, are you kidding?"

She shrugs.

He puts the paper down on the counter, comes over to her, takes her face between his large hands. "The instant I saw you."

"Well," she says, laughing a little.

"Don't you know that?"

"Well, I thought so."

"Haven't I told you a million times?"

"I guess you have, Robert."

"She was a vision in blue," he tells me.

"Yellow," my mother says.

"Whatever," my father says, continuing to look at me. His eyes narrow. "There was not a doubt in my mind. I had to have her." He turns back to my mother. "And I got her! Didn't I?"

"Yes you did, Robert."

"Didn't I?"

"Yes."

"All right." He kisses her, then goes back to the counter, retrieves his newspaper. "What's for dinner?"

"Salmon."

"And?"

"Red potatoes, green beans, carrots, a nice salad."

"And?"

"No, Robert."

"Not even sorbet?"

"Not tonight."

"She's killing me," he tells me. "But I did fall in love with her at first sight." He stretches, scratches lazily at his side. "Anything else?"

"No, Dad."

"All right. I'm busy, then."

My mother and I look at each other, smile.

Everything they have, I want. I know that when he puts his hands to her face, she recognizes his smell, claims the larger part of his history. I can't stand it that they still blush around each other. Their love seems at times to have weight and take up space. Like matter. Like what matters.

My mother resumes peeling carrots. I sigh loudly.

"What?" she says.

"You and Dad. Sometimes it's sort of depressing to be around you."

She looks up.

"No, it's . . . You know, you're just so right for each other."

"That will come to you, too."

I look out the window. The wind has picked up. "I don't know."

"It will," my mother says. "It will happen when you're not looking for it to. Love likes to take you by surprise. And anyway, you're just . . . *des*tined to get married and have children. I knew it about you from the time you were a little girl. I could tell from the way you played dolls—you were a natural. You'll make a wonderful mother."

"Oh, we all played dolls. Even Johnny, remember? He took my Betsy-Wetsy to school with him on the first day of kindergarten."

"Yes, and you were so furious at him."

"Well, there was finger paint all over her when he brought her home!"

"It washed out."

"Not from her sunsuit. And that was her favorite sunsuit."

My mother reaches across the table, touches my face. "You see what I mean, then."

I look away, remembering my life as mother to Betsy. How she slept in a crib my father made her, covered with an afghan my mother had knitted. How I would wake up sometimes at night and turn on my light to look down at her. I truly thought she might have awakened and be looking up at me, asking for something I was entirely ready to give. Even then. Truly, even then.

I played a lot of games growing up: jacks, Mother, May I?, hide-and-seek, endless rounds of Monopoly that went on for entire Christmas vacations. I dressed unfortunate kittens in doll dresses with round collars and short, puffy sleeves before I gave them a ride on the swing.

I also did things like ring doorbells and run away, and call strangers to ask, "Is your refrigerator running?" I explored half-built houses and swamps with water thick as stew, though my hands were held in close to me at those times, and a pastel ribbon usually fluttered in my hair, announcing my not-really-tomboy status. I walked down storm drains until I got scared I'd gone too far in; then, thrilled to the bone by visions of drowning, I'd run out. I scaled the fierce-looking but easily climbed fence at the transportation department in order to slide down the huge piles of sand stored there, until I heard that a kid had suffocated doing that. He was a kid who also had epilepsy; everyone in my small gang met at our clubhouse—a deserted garage furnished with an army blanket, cardboard boxes, and Oreos—to discuss the scary unfairness of the situation.

But it was always dolls I liked playing with the best. I treated them with great respect: washed their little dresses in a dishpan out on the front porch, hung them out to dry, then ironed and folded them and put them away in their Whitman's candy-box bureaus. I never cut their hair into fright wigs like all my other friends did with their dolls. I heard about one girl who dumped catsup all over her life-sized doll, then put her in the bushes and waited for someone to come along and start screaming. That news depressed me. If I'd known where the horrible event occurred, I would have gone over to rescue the doll immediately, would have tenderly bathed her and then dressed her in the finest outfit I owned, my First Communion ensemble. That sparkly white dress and veil lived in a plastic bag in my closet for years, making my other clothes feel guilty.

It's true that I had a particular passion for Betsy-Wetsy; but I loved all my dolls, the baby dolls especially, with their sweetly needy faces and uncomplaining dispositions. Not that I didn't understand what the real deal was with babies—my younger siblings showed me what red-faced squalling and leaky diapers were all about. But I wanted this. On one inspired occasion I put scrambled eggs in my dolls' diapers. Then I carefully pinned the diapers back on, went away to attend to some task, and later came back into the room to wave the air before my nose and say, "Oh, my goodness! *What* have we got in-a *britch*es?" which is, of course, exactly what my mother said.

I imagined the baby dolls' sweet smiles replaced by mouths open and trembling in baby rage; and at those times I swaddled the dolls in receiving blankets and paced and patted and sighed wearily and worried mightily and felt satisfied to the core.

I played dolls until I was fourteen, and only stopped then because I was too afraid someone would catch me, and I would be embarrassed for the rest of my life. I would play dolls now if anyone would play seriously with me. Once, when Ethan and I were dating, I showed him my doll collection and we played a bit. He was very good at it. But we were both a little drunk; it didn't count.

I also loved playing house. I thought domesticity was a many-splendored thing; I didn't know what could possibly be more satisfying than looking in the Sears catalogue for a new club chair while pineapple-upside-down cake baked in the oven. I liked all the trappings of the modern home: the steam iron, the copper-bottomed pots and pans, the scientifically engineered cleaning products, the pull-out vegetable bin of the frost-free refrigerator. I liked TV trays and paper doilies and the stately Mixmaster.

I learned to make chocolate-chip cookies by the time I was seven and it gave me a real sense of power. "Please, *please*!" my little brother and sisters would clamor when I removed the cookies from the baking trays to store them in the cookie jar. "No sweets until after dinner," I would say, prim-mouthed, and then, finally, "Oh all right, but just *one*." My mother's white ruffled apron hung low on me, swayed languidly over my official Brownie oxfords. I was a model of cheerful righteousness and authority. I thought all you needed was a husband, a house, children, and a decent oven, and you could be happy. I still think that. It's just that now I'm afraid to admit it.

I finish with my carrots, and look up to see my mother staring at me, smiling.

"What?" I say. I still hate it when she catches me daydreaming.

"Nothing. You're all right."

"I know," I say. And then, standing, "Well, okay. I think I'm going to go."

"You don't want to stay for dinner?"

"No, I don't like salmon."

"Is that right?"

"You know that, Mom."

She turns in her chair, yells, "Robert?"

Nothing.

"*ROB*ert?"

A moment. Then, "WHAT?"

"PATTY'S *LEAV*ING!"

"Ma," I say. "Stop yelling! I can go into the den and tell him myself. Jesus. It's like boot camp around here."

She smacks me on the butt. "Don't swear."

"I just said 'Jesus.' It's not like I said—"

"Don't start. Honestly. You're just like your father."

Who has appeared, again with newspaper in hand. "You're leaving?"

"Yeah. I'll see you later." I cross the room to kiss him. He smells like a cigar. In anyone else, I would hate this.

"You don't like salmon?" he asks.

"She doesn't like salmon," my mother says.

"Why not?"

"Dad."

"Why *not?*"

"Jesus," I sigh.

"*Pa*tty," my mother says. And then, to my father, "She just doesn't *like* it, Robert."

"What?"

"Salmon!"

"Well, I know that, Marilyn. She just said that. So. What should we do tonight?" My father is finished with me.

"I don't know." My mother wipes her hands on her apron, starts filling the kitchen sink with dish soap and water. She looks over at him. "Go to a movie?"

"Why don't we go to a movie?"

"All right, Robert."

"Good." He looks at me over his glasses. "Come on, Scout. I'll walk you out to the car."

He calls me this, sometimes, "Scout." I don't know why. I am also Poker Chip and Bean Blossom. And on occasion, Fruit Toots. I always want these nicknames. I never want anyone else to know them, though.

When I open the car door and sit down, my father leans in and kisses my forehead. "I'm a little worried about your mother," he says.

I feel the dull sock of alarm to my stomach. "Why?"

"She's . . . I don't know, kind of depressed. I think it's the menopause got her again."

"It doesn't get you twice, Dad."

"Well, she's acting just like she did then."

"Huh." I can't think of anything to say. I hadn't noticed. Plus I don't want to worry about my mother. I'm too consumed with myself.

"Don't worry about her," my father says, as though he were reading my mind.

"Just . . . call if you need me," I say.

"I'll call you if I need you."

"All right, Dad."

"How would that be?"

"That would be fine."

Everything has to be his idea. It's always been that way. But you can't help but like him anyway. You can't help but love him.

I watch him standing in the driveway, holding his paper, as I pull away. I raise my hand until I see him do it too. Then I head back to my pretend home while my father goes into his real one.

6

On Saturday afternoon, Mark comes over to install the VCR someone at work gave me. Sally Gunderson sells a house a week, it seems like. She's rolling in dough, and she's always buying something new and giving away the old one. I have a bread maker from her that she got rid of because it didn't have a timer. Also a quilt whose colors she decided she wasn't crazy about. I hope the sale she's working on now goes through; maybe she'll give me her house.

Mark is very good at this, as most men are. He has the VCR up and running in almost no time, and we put in the movie we rented. It's *Moonstruck,* a compromise, because I wanted Bette Davis and he wanted Sly Stallone. Ethan will always watch Bette Davis.

Cher is kissing Nicolas Cage when Mark takes my hand. So gently. If I were watching him in a movie, I'd think, what a great guy. And he is a great guy. For anyone but me. I don't know why his hand wrapped around mine makes me feel like someone is holding me down. I am finding it hard to breathe. I am thinking, What can I do that will make me need to get up?

And now he is turning my face toward him and kissing me and I feel that as soon as he stops I'll start screaming. I don't, of course. I say, "Would you like some pretzels?"

Later, after a long walk, we are out for ice-cream sundaes. I liked the walk. That part, I liked.

"I can't believe you don't like chocolate ice cream," Mark says.

"I know," I say. "It annoys everyone. They seem to take it personally. But I only like vanilla."

"Try this, though," he says, holding a spoonful of his sundae toward me.

"I don't want it," I say. "Thanks."

"Just *try,*" he says.

"It's no *use*!"

"Pardon?"

"I don't like chocolate ice cream." I take a big bite of my sundae, then point to it with my spoon, saying, "This is good. *This* is what I like."

"Okay." He looks away, flushes slightly. I don't know why people get so upset that I don't like chocolate ice cream. This has been going on since I was a child, when I also detested hot dogs. "You don't *like* them????" kids would say at parties, at picnics, waving their wieners in front of my face. "*These,* you don't *like*????"

"*No*!" I would say, "I don't *like* them!" Then I would eat the bun with catsup and mustard and relish on it, saying it was fine. And it was.

By the time we've finished our sundaes, Mark still hasn't

looked at me. I suppose I've really pissed him off. I excuse myself and go to the ladies' room. When I come out of the stall to wash my hands, I look up into the mirror. There, at the side of my mouth and extending up toward my nose, I see a smear of caramel. I look quickly around the washroom, grateful that it's empty. Then I wash the smear off. It takes a little scrubbing.

When I rejoin Mark, he smiles and says, "Ah. You fixed it."

"Yeah," I say. But what's in my head is: I don't think so.

"It's not working," I tell Ethan on the phone. "But he's wonderful."

"Patty," Ethan sighs. "Think about what you just said."

"I know. I know! But he's not for me, that's all."

"You just have to give things a little time."

"I have!"

"Three weeks?"

"Three weeks of intensive dating."

"Three weeks of playing around. Try a real date. Dress up like a big girl. Have some sex. Both of you need to relax!"

"What do you mean? What does he say about me? What?"

"Nothing."

"Oh, please."

"Nothing but good things, which I'm not going to tell you because you're a nasty person who doesn't deserve to hear them."

"I'm not nasty!"

Silence.

"Ethan, just because you failed as a matchmaker—"

"I didn't fail."

“See? This is why you should never get fixed up by friends. If you don’t like who they pick out, they get all pissed off.”

“You really don’t like him?”

“Well . . . no. I do *like* him.”

“So give it some time, Patty!”

“Fine,” I say, and lie back on the sofa, look up at the ceiling. Flat. No color there, really.

The next Saturday evening, I’m getting ready to go out to dinner with Mark. This time it’s to a real restaurant, some fancy place in Boston near the Common, to celebrate our one-month “anniversary.” He won’t tell me where. I have to say I love these kinds of corny surprises. I always wanted to bite into a dinner roll and find my engagement ring. This actually happened to a friend of mine. She and her boyfriend were eating one of those box dinners from Kentucky Fried Chicken and she bit into her roll and—voilà! “What if I had eaten it?” she asked him, and he said he hadn’t thought of that. Good thing she hadn’t. She brushed the crumbs off the ring, and put it on her finger. A few years later, they were divorced. Both of them had decided they were gay. True story. They now live with same-sex partners. But they’ve remained very good friends. True story.

I bought a new dress this afternoon at Theresa’s, a long red one with a slit up the side. Then I went over to Elaine’s to borrow her red Wonder Bra. “You actually wear this?” I asked, watching the stuffed cups rotate lazily as the thing dangled from my hand.

“Never for very long, if you know what I mean.”

“Oh. Well, is it . . . clean?”

She rolled her eyes.

"Is it?" I asked and she said, "*Yes,* it's clean!" And then she told me to try it on and I had to admit that it did have a certain . . . allure. "Wow," I said quietly, staring into the dresser mirror at myself.

"See?" Elaine said. "Doesn't it even turn *you* on?" She was lying on her bed with a fat novel, dressed in jeans and a long-sleeved T-shirt under a plaid flannel shirt. She had a little cold, the satisfying kind where your voice is affected so people feel sorry for you but you secretly feel fine. She was going to stay in tonight, order a double cheese pizza and read until ten o'clock, when *All About Eve* came on. I envied her.

"I don't want to go," I said, sitting on the bed beside her. I saw my breasts jiggle like Jell-O in their Wonder Bra serving cups. It was a little sickening.

"Why not?"

"I don't know."

"Oh, you're just nervous. You always get nervous when you have to dress up."

"True. But it's more than that."

"Well, yeah. Tonight's the night, right?"

I look at her. I'm tired, I realize. I need a little nap. Fifteen, sixteen hours or so.

"Isn't it?"

"I don't know."

"Patty. You came over here all excited. What just happened?"

"I don't know."

"Will you please find something else to say?"

"Well, I *don't* know, Elaine! I just . . . something's missing, okay? It's just not right. I had a lot of hope this time. I tried. But it's just not *right*."

"Listen to me. Don't blow this. He is the best thing you've had happen in a long time. Ever, in fact. And he's crazy about you!"

"Yeah." I really want to say "I don't know."

"He's got everything you could want. He's good-looking, he's smart, he's got a good job, he has a HUGE feminine side."

"What do you mean?"

"You know what I mean. He's sensitive. Intuitive. Imaginative. He actually listens, too, right?"

I sigh. It's true. I should never have told Elaine all the good things Mark does. I never dreamed she'd use them against me this way. There is nothing bad I can find to say about Mark. And yet.

Oh, who can account for these things? I had a friend who was wild about a guy I simply could not understand her attraction to. Once, over a drink, I asked her what she saw in him. She said it was his smell. "His cologne?" I asked, and she said no, the smell you weren't aware of smelling. Chemistry, I guess she meant. It's a powerful thing. A guy can be a real asshole, but if he's got the right pheromones, we hand over our hearts. Similarly, a guy can do everything right, and if it isn't there, well, by God, it just isn't there. And the more you try to force it, the worse it gets. It never, never works to try to talk yourself into someone. What happens is not that you gradually start to fall in love with him. What happens is that you see him take the cap off his fountain pen and think, What a jerk. You lie in your bathtub getting ready for yet another date with him, and as you're washing under your arms you stare into space and say quietly, "Fuck you, I hate this." Then you let the water drain out of the tub and then you put your makeup on so he'll think you're pretty.

"Hey, wake up!" Elaine hits me with her book, and I take it from her, start thumbing through the pages. "Is this good?"

She grabs the book away from me. "Go home and get in a better mood. You're going out to dinner with a very good man, and you're going to look fabulous, thanks to me; and you're going to have fun, and when you come home you have every chance of having great sex, which, I must say, you NEED."

"I don't know."

"Go home."

"Okay. Elaine?"

"Yeah?"

"Do you really think that much of him?"

She starts to say something, stops. Then, "Yeah," she says. "If it weren't you . . ."

"What? If it weren't me, what?"

"I'd try . . . I'd give you some competition."

"You would?"

"Yeah."

"*You'd* want him?"

"Yeah!"

"Huh. Maybe I won't invite you over anymore when he's there."

She lies back on her bed, stretches prettily. "He doesn't go for me."

"How do you know?"

"I can tell."

"Of course he does. Every man does."

"Not him. It's you he's interested in."

"Huh," I said. And said again, a few times, on the way home.

So tonight may be the night. It may be. I do a little imaginative run-through in my mind, see Mark and me in my bed together, then in his. It is like ordering bacon and eggs and not getting the bacon. You stare at the plate, thinking, Ah, jeez.

I put on my earrings, stand back to see how they look. It's probably just that it's been too long. I'm protecting myself, maybe that's it.

The phone rings. After I say hello, there is a silence.

"If this is an obscene phone call, please try me at a more convenient time," I say. "I'm in a hurry." And then, " . . . Elaine?"

A ragged intake of breath. It *is* an obscene phone call! I hang up. The phone rings again. I pick it up and say, "I have caller ID." A lie.

"Well, good for you," Ethan says.

"Ethan! Do you have a cold?"

"No."

"Oh. Well . . . Are you *crying*?"

Silence.

"What happened?"

"Elton Jane died. She died. Today. In the vet's office."

"Oh, Ethan. I'm sorry."

"I wasn't even there." He blows his nose. "I can't believe I'm this upset."

"Well, you loved her. People get very attached to their pets. Very attached. There are pet *bereavement* groups."

"There are?"

"Yes."

"Where?"

"Well, I don't know, Ethan, I've just read about them."

"I can't tell you how . . . The worst thing is, she didn't *know.*"

I look at my watch, then at my other clocks. Three minutes to Mark.

"What didn't she know, Ethan?"

"She didn't know I was on my way, I was coming, I wanted to be there with her. Instead, she died before I got there, in some fucking *cage.*"

"Well . . . She had a very good life with you, Ethan."

"She was a great cat. Such a great cat."

Well.

"And she was so smart! Did you know she used to meow to go out? And those tinfoil balls I used to make her? She saved them. She had a pile in the closet. And also, every time the phone rang, she ran to it."

He waits. For me, I presume, to make my contribution to this impromptu memorial service.

"She was really . . . white," I say. "Really, very . . . pretty." I begrudge that cat a single kind word. Even in death.

"Yeah, she was beautiful." His voice is quivery. It sounds a little like he's singing.

I hear my doorbell ring.

"Ethan? Mark's just come, we were going out to dinner."

"Oh, really? Where?" His voice has changed. He's back to the business of being my social secretary.

"Someplace in Boston, near the Common. I don't know which restaurant, it's a surprise."

"Oh, I know what one. I told him about it. I went last week, it's fabulous." He sniffs.

"Do you . . . do you want to come?"

"No. No, of course not. Go let him in."

"Oh! Right. Hold on."

I open the door, see Mark standing there, smiling. And am suddenly furious at him that he is not furious at me for having to wait so long.

"I can't go," I say.

"What?"

"I can't go. Ethan's on the phone. Somebody died."

"Oh, God, really?"

"Yeah. I'm sorry. I need to go and see him. . . . You look great."

He laughs. "So do you."

"We could . . . you want to go another time?"

"Sure."

"Okay, we will. We will. Soon. I'll call you, okay?"

"Sure." He kisses me lightly, starts to walk away, then turns back. "Patty?"

"Yeah?"

"Who died?"

I don't say anything.

"Besides us, I mean."

Again, I say nothing. I feel terrible. And so relieved. Then, "I'm sorry," I say.

He nods, disappears down the sidewalk into the darkness.

I pick up the phone. "Ethan?"

"I heard that. You didn't have to do that."

"But I did. I . . . there's something wrong with me." I start crying. "Oh, Ethan, he was just *fine.* He was wonderful. And probably my last chance. There's something really, really wrong with me."

"Oh, I don't know, maybe I'll come over. Should I come over?"

"Okay."

I am such a bad person. My spirits are just soaring.

"Wow," Ethan says, when I open the door.

"Well."

He eyes my cleavage. "Are you . . . is that *you*?"

"Wonder Bra. It's Elaine's."

"Ah."

"Is it gross?"

"No, it's . . . wondrous."

"Thank you."

"So." He hangs up his coat, goes over to the refrigerator. "What do you have in the way of grief food?"

"Raw cookie dough?"

". . . umm . . ."

"We could make some mashed potatoes."

"Yes. *Garlic* mashed." He closes the refrigerator door, takes a Dutch oven out of my cupboard. I take out a sack of potatoes, a head of beautiful garlic. It is complete, ours for the having.

"Patty?"

"Yeah?"

"Change your dress."

"I was going to," I say. But I wasn't. I'd forgotten all about it.

When the potatoes are done, we sit shoulder to shoulder on the sofa, watching TV and talking and eating out of the pan with my biggest serving spoons. It is very, very good.

We are getting ready to watch a movie when my mother calls to tell me my brother's wife is pregnant again. I tell her that's wonderful, the usual drill, quash the ache of jealousy inside myself. Then, "Can I call you back tomorrow?" I say. "We were just going to watch something—it's starting in a minute."

"Oh, sure. Tell Mark I said hello."

"Well, it's . . . not Mark. It's Ethan."

"Didn't you tell me you had a date with Mark tonight?"

"Yes, I did."

"But Ethan's there?"

"You know what, Mom?" I say. "It's starting right now. I'll call you tomorrow."

I hang up the phone.

"My mom says hello," I tell Ethan.

He nods, smiles; then leans back into the sofa, his hands clasped behind his head, his feet up on the table. His socks are a beige mini-print, lovely to behold. I watch them as much as the movie.

In the morning, I call Elaine. "Guess what?"

"You broke up with Mark."

"How do you know?"

"He called me."

A moment.

"He did?"

"Yeah. To find out what the deal is with you."

"What did you tell him?"

"I said I didn't know. And I swear to God, I don't know."

"Yes, you do."

"What, you love *Ethan*?"

"Yes. Yes, I do."

"Patty, you need to stop this. It's . . . an excuse or something. What is the point in wasting so much energy on someone who is never, ever going to love you back? Cut your losses and move *on*."

"Fuck you, Elaine."

She hangs up.

I call her back.

"Don't hang up on me," I say. "I need you."

"Then don't abuse me."

"I'm not abusing you. It's just . . . Ethan and me. You don't understand. If I could just . . . Listen, I want to tell you something." I sit down, cross my legs, lower my voice. "Ethan's cat died, and he hasn't had sex with anyone for over a year."

"Pretty extreme reaction."

"No, his cat died and he came over because he felt terrible and we were just, you know, really talking, and he told me he hasn't had sex in over a year!"

"And you told Mark to kiss off."

"Not really." I don't know why she wants to talk about this. That is not why I called her.

"You did, Patty! He comes over to take you out to this fabulous place and you tell him to get lost. Because Ethan's *cat* died."

"Well, for Christ's sake, Elaine, why are you taking this so personally? I don't have to love Mark, just because you could!"

Silence. I play with the phone cord a little, then stop.

"Elaine?"

"What?"

"Could you?"

"Maybe I could."

"Well . . . so . . . take him."

"He's not a *thing* that you hand back and forth, Patty!"

"I know. But I'm sure if he knew you were interested—"

"He knows, okay?"

"You told him last night?"

"I told him before last night."

"You did?"

"In so many words."

"Wow." This is not exactly what I mean. Well, you *bitch*! is what I mean.

"Sorry," she says.

"And he didn't . . . ?"

"That's what you threw away."

Now I hang up. In my head, I see some random woman in some random '40s film. She is sitting at a restaurant table with another woman. "Did you get a load of that?" she is saying. "Boy, you think you know someone." Her hat is on a little crooked. The stream of cigarette smoke she blows hard out of her mouth is dead straight on, however.

7

I am out in the backyard of an empty three-bedroom colonial trying to entertain the five-year-old son of my clients, the Dugans, who are inside fighting. He wants it. She doesn't. This is a waste of time. If the She doesn't want it, you can count on the couple not buying it. The She has to want it. If the He doesn't want it, nine times out of ten it's almost irrelevant; the She will talk him into it. But if the She doesn't want it, forget it. Still, I told the Dugans to take some time, I'd be outside in the backyard when they were ready. It's a nice winter day—bright sun, temperature in the mid-forties. The son's name is Charles. Not Charlie, he informs me.

"I wasn't going to call you Charlie," I say.

"Everybody does."

"Well, I wasn't. You look like a Charles."

He eyes me suspiciously. He's an ugly child, which normally attracts me, but not in this case. The kid's stuck-up. Bratty. When we looked at the house before this one, it was all I could do not to escort him from the place. Firmly. He was offering a running commentary in front of the owners: everything was stupid. At least he was succinct.

"What does a Charles look like?" he asks now.

"Well, sort of . . . royal. Do you know who Prince Charles is?"

He shakes his head no.

"Prince Charles, of England?"

He shrugs.

"Well, you remind me of him. He's quite . . . aristocratic-looking. And a good gardener. Do you like gardens?"

He sighs. "When are we leaving? This is boring."

"Your parents wanted to talk about the house a little bit, remember?"

He turns, looks back toward it.

"Do you like it? Did you like what would be your bedroom?"

"No, it's stupid."

"Hey, Charles," I say. "What's *not* stupid?"

"Not *you.*"

"Okay."

"Not *you* are not stupid."

"Yes, I understood."

He scowls, sits down on the light covering of snow. His shoulders slump; then he kicks his heels against the ground in a half-hearted fit.

"Do you know you're kind of a brat?" I say. I don't care; this couple will never buy anything.

He looks up.

"Yes," I say. "You are. If you were older, you'd be an asshole."

I see the couple emerging from the backdoor.

"Mooooommmmm!" Charles yells, running to her. "She called me an asshole!"

The woman, Joanne her name is, regards me from under lifted brows.

"Sorry," I say. And am not surprised when they ask that I drive them back to the office. But I am surprised when they simply drive away. I thought they were going to tell on me. And I'd get fired. Which might be a relief. And would not particularly matter, since I'm in such a bad mood all the time anyway, lately. Everything in my life is wrong except that Elaine and I finally made up. Sort of. She's really sorry. I have kind of forgiven her.

There is a message on my desk from the Berkenheimers. I call them back, and Muriel answers.

"Patty!" she says. "How nice to hear your voice."

"Yours, too," I say, and it's true.

A long silence, and then Muriel says, "So? What can I do for you?"

"Oh! Well, I had a message that *you* called."

"You did? I didn't call. Wait a minute." I hear her cover the phone, then yell, "Artie? Did you call Patty Murphy? Patty Murphy's on the phone, did you call her?"

A moment, and then there is Artie's voice, saying, "I'll call you right back."

"Okay," I say. And hang up. And wait for about twenty minutes, without getting any phone calls. And then I leave for my manicure, which will be the only good thing that has happened to me for many, many days.

• • •

"Don't start telling me how unrealistic I am," I tell Amber.

She looks up. "Did I say anything?"

"Not yet."

"I'm not going to say anything like that. Listen, what are you going to do? We love who we love."

"I wish you'd tell my mother that. When I told her I'd stopped seeing Mark, she threw a dinner roll at me." And delivered a loud lecture about how she had been patient, but what in hell was I waiting for? My father put his hand over hers, and she pulled it away. "She's ruining her *life*!" she told him.

"Okay, Marilyn," he'd said.

"Well she is! Someone has got to tell her!"

"Okay."

"Mom," I said. "You don't understand. When I kissed him, it was like watching someone else do it."

"I don't think I need to hear any of these personal details, Patty."

"But you do! Don't you see how lucky you were? Don't you see how hard it is to find what you found?"

"Well, now, she's got a point there, Marilyn," my father said.

She got up, started bussing dishes angrily.

"Mom!" I said. "Why are you so *angry*?"

"Marilyn!" my father said.

She turned to him. "What?!"

"I'm not done!"

He pointed to the half-full plate she had in her hand.

She gave it back to him, then left the room.

"Jesus," I said, extremely quietly.

My father raised his eyebrows, stared at me over his glasses. "This is what I mean. Lately, she'll fly right off the handle, just like that. Ten or fifteen minutes go by, she's fine again." He reached across me for another dinner roll. It made him grunt a little, doing it.

"I can't do it, Dad. I can't stay in a relationship just because the guy looks good on paper."

"You don't have to, honey."

"Well, she seems to think—"

"She's worried about you. She wants you to be happy. She wants you to have a baby before it's too late. Not that it's anywhere near too late, Scout, you've got lots of time. Lots of time." He buttered a roll. Generously.

"Dad."

"Yeah?"

"Since when do you use butter?"

"Shh!"

"But your—"

"Listen, kiddo. You make the most out of a situation, you know?"

I said nothing.

"Am I right?"

"Okay," I said. And then, "Dad? I don't really have a lot of time."

"Well." He put his roll down, took my hand. "I know."

Now Amber says, "I don't blame you for honoring your true feelings. It's very important to do that. I know too many people who tried to talk themselves into love and then suffered terribly for it. Terribly." She squints at a nick in my thumbnail, tsks, sighs, starts filing it smooth.

"How?"

"What?"

"How did they suffer?"

She stares at me blankly.

"The people who tried to talk themselves into it. Into love. How did they suffer?"

"Oh. Well, I don't really know anyone like that. I was just trying to make you feel better." She shrugs, cracks her gum.

"I just don't know what to do anymore."

"Hey. Get a cat. You know? People who live with cats are 70 percent happier than those who live with people."

"That's not true!"

"I swear to God."

"That can't be true."

"It is. Dogs, 40 percent."

I stop talking, take some comfort from the sounds of female chatter and blow-dryers. I watch a very thin young woman dressed entirely in black use a wide broom to clean up varying shades of hair. It's probably all married hair. I look around at the women in the place. Yup, nearly all of them wear wedding rings.

"I am incapable of having a meaningful relationship," I tell Amber. "That's it. It's a very interesting form of self-sabotage, because what I want most in my life is to have a family. But every time I get anywhere close, I make sure to mess it up. Now why do I do that?"

Amber sits back in her chair. "This is a nine-dollar manicure. You know?"

"I'm sorry."

"What color do you want?"

"You pick."

She selects a bottle of colorless polish.

"What, are you mad at me?"

She smiles, shakes her head. "I think you've got that all taken care of, hon. No, you don't get color because your nails look like shit. Have you been biting them?"

"No!"

"You can tell me."

"A little."

"Well, cut it out."

"Okay."

She starts painting my thumbnail.

"The problem is, I'm in love with a gay man," I say quietly.

"I know," she says. Not quietly.

I am getting pretty tired of telling this story. But not nearly as tired as people are of hearing it.

Back at the office, there is another message from Artie. This time he answers. "Is that cottage on Green Street still for sale?" His voice is low, secretive.

"Yes, I think so. You want to see it again?"

"No, I want to buy it."

"But don't you want to see it again first? It was a few months ago—"

"No, I want to buy it. I got the money. What do we need to do?"

"Well, we'll need to make an offer first, see what they come back with."

"Give them full price."

"Oh, I don't think you—"

"Give them full price, I'll be in tomorrow, we'll do the paperwork."

"All right. But you'll have to give me a check with the offer. A thousand dollars. Earnest money. You know."

"Oh yeah, right. I forgot about that. Been a long time since I bought a house. How late are you there?"

"I can meet you anytime, Artie."

"All right. Eight o'clock tonight."

"Is Muriel coming?"

"No."

I'd thought not.

I think about Artie handing me the earnest money and I get a notion, suddenly, that it will be cash. Out of a coffee can. A big stack of dollar bills, bent in half, or maybe rolled up in a rubber band that Muriel took off a bunch of celery long ago. And then I get another notion. That, taking that money, I'll feel really bad.

The phone rings again. Mrs. Dugan. Could they see the colonial again, tonight? Sure, I say, surprised. She tells me they'll be there in twenty minutes.

An hour later, I am sitting on the kitchen floor of the colonial, admiring my manicure, looking in my purse to see if there's anything I can play with in there. Nothing. Once more, I go to the window to look out and see if there are any cars coming. No. Well, this could be a couple of things. It could be that Joanne is paying me back for calling her kid an asshole. Or it could be that she just won't show up. This happens all the time in real estate. You show up somewhere, the clients don't.

I turn out the kitchen light, then walk around the house, turning out all the other lights. Then, in the beautiful light of the full moon outside, I pretend I live here. I go to the door of a bedroom, lean in. "Good night," I say. The boy, Lego creations lined up on the windowsill. Then I go to another bedroom door, lean in that one, say, "Good niiiiight." The girl, irresistible dresses hanging in her closet, though she prefers her bib overalls. On which I have embroidered things. Little flowers. A sun with a face.

I go down into the kitchen, open the empty ice box. "Hon?" I say. "I'm making a sandwich. Do you want one?"

I close the refrigerator door, lean against it, sigh. I have books on the shelves of the little den; I have a sewing basket in the family room; I have miniature marshmallows in the cupboard. I have whimsically decorated Band-Aids in the medicine chest: cartoon figures, stars, glitter. I have a kitchen calendar with writing all over it. Every day, there are human events for which I am responsible. Things done by and for the children I made, the husband who loves me.

"Wait for me, okay?" I call out. I'm talking to my husband who wants to start the movie we rented. I think that's who I'm talking to.

Back at the office, I turn on the lights and call the answering service. Dugans called. Sorry they missed me. But right before our appointment, they decided on another house. Uh-huh. And Muriel Berkenheimer. What in the hell is going on with them?

I dial their number. Muriel answers.

"It's Patty," I say.

"Oh, Patty." She starts to cry.

"Muriel?"

"Can you come over?"

"I—come over to your house?"

"Yes, it's not so far. Thirty, thirty-five minutes. Have you had dinner?"

"Well, no, actually."

"So you'll come, we'll have some dinner. We have to talk."

"Muriel, did Artie—"

"I know, Patty. Come over. We'll talk."

8

Artie and Muriel live in a small but thoroughly charming Cape. When Muriel opens the door and shows me into the living room, I see gorgeous moldings, a fireplace with a carved mantel, a fire burning there. The furniture is exactly what I might have envisioned for them: Sears-type colonial, the upholstery shades of green and rust. A maple coffee table is crowded with photographs, and there is a candy dish full of butterscotch. The lamps remind me of the extravagant hats worn by Victorian women. I can smell beef roasting, and it comes to me that it's been a long time since I've smelled that most substantial of smells.

"Came for dinner, huh?" Artie asks, rising up out of his recliner to greet me.

"Yes, Muriel was kind enough to invite me. It smells great, too."

"It's just pot roast," Muriel says. "It's nothing. Although it was a very nice cut, I must say. You have to ask the butcher, they keep the best stuff in the back, I have no idea why."

"Their families," Artie says.

"What?" Muriel holds her hand out for my coat, and I give it to her.

"It's for their *families,* they keep it back there for their families."

Muriel stares at him. "What would you know about it? When was the last time you shopped? If it weren't for me, you'd never eat." She looks at me. "If it weren't for me, he'd never eat."

"You just *said* that, Muriel, what do you think, the girl doesn't hear? You think she's deaf?"

"I was telling *her,*" Muriel says. "First I was just *saying,* then I was telling her specifically. You don't mind, do you, Patty?"

I smile, shake my head no.

"You see?" she asks Artie.

"I see, Muriel." He sits back down.

Artie's lost weight—his knit-shirt collar gapes around his neck. It is, as usual, buttoned all the way up to the top. He wears a lime green cardigan that looks like a golf sweater, brown pants belted high, leather slippers. Muriel wears slippers, too, a fleece-lined type that look warm and comfortable and very old. This is my idea of a good way to spend married life: in your house that is just big enough, a fire going, dinner in the oven, and slippers on your feet. And a sure love, regardless of the form it takes.

"People like to be addressed specifically, Artie, it makes them feel important," Muriel says.

Artie sighs. "She never stops."

Muriel might have lost weight, too. Her face looks thinner. Or maybe it's just that she's tired. There are bags under her eyes.

She hangs up my coat in the tiny hall closet. Then, hands clasped nervously in front of her, she asks, "Would you like a drink?"

"A drink?"

"Yeah, you know, a cocktail."

"I can make you a martini that'll curl you hair," Artie says. Then, looking at my hair, "More."

"Okay. I've never had one."

"You're kidding!" Muriel says. And then, to Artie, "Can you believe it? She's never had a martini!"

"Come on down to my bar," Artie says, "I'll fix you right up."

I follow him through the dining room, where our places are set with china, with flowered cloth napkins. Two forks! Then through the warm kitchen to the basement door. "Come right back up," Muriel tells us, manning her position in front of the stove. "I'm starting the gravy right now. And I don't want things to get cold."

Gravy! My spirits lift like a dog's head when he hears the word *out*. Gravy is something single people don't make. It's something my mother never makes anymore, either, because of my father's severely restricted diet. If there's gravy, surely the potatoes will be browned and crisp at the edges, the carrots curled, the onions softened into a yellow sweetness that can be spread on bread like butter.

"Ta-da!" Artie says, turning on a light switch that bathes a corner of the basement—his bar—with a pinkish neon light. This must have been his paradise, at one time. Perhaps it still is. The bar is huge, a burgundy Naugahyde with diamond-shaped tufting accented by round gold studs. There are six stools, their padded seats also burgundy Naugahyde, rips in two of them inexpertly repaired with silver duct tape. Next to the bar is a wooden clothes rack draped with Muriel's flag-sized underpants and industrial-strength bras. Artie moves it to the other side of the basement. I wonder why she air-dries her lingerie; it looks as though it could withstand being laundered on rocks at the river.

"Now!" Artie rubs his hands together briskly, then goes behind the bar. "Used to be the hot spot of the neighborhood," he says. " 'Artie's place,' we called it. We had parties down here almost every weekend."

Along the back wall of the bar a smoke-colored mirror veined with gold reflects a bit of fringe on the back of Artie's head; his baldness shines above it. He turns on a phonograph, puts on an album, and Sinatra begins singing, "The Lady Is a Tramp." Artie sings along under his breath so wildly off-key I think maybe he's joking, but when I look at him closely I see he is not. He reaches under the bar for glasses, raises his eyebrows up and down at me. It is the fifties; he is Hugh Heffner. Then, looking at the dust on the glasses, he says, "Well. Let me just wash these off first." It is the nineties; he is Artie Berkenheimer, who carries two bottles of pills in his front shirt pocket. Sometimes they click together, making a sound like ill-fitting dentures.

"Two MINutes!" Muriel screams down the stairs.

"Oy." Artie turns his back to me to pull down bottles of liquor from the shelf above the mirror. He nudges the phonograph so Frank stops skipping, then opens the little refrigerator for ice, dumps some into a tall silver shaker. "Been a long time since I drank anything but seltzer down here," he says. But his movements are smooth and practiced; it's like watching a real bartender.

I look around a little, see a weight bench and some barbells in another dim corner of the basement.

"Do you work out?" I ask.

He looks across the room, smiles. "Years ago," he says. "I had a little book, charts and everything. Jack La Lanne. You measured yourself once a week—biceps, abdomen. Thighs." He shrugs. "I don't know what happened, why I stopped. Maybe I hurt myself. I don't remember, it was a long time ago." He goes back to making drinks. I settle back on the bar stool, cross my legs. "So," I say.

"So." He doesn't turn around.

"So you really want to buy that cottage, huh?"

He sets two glasses and the shaker on the counter before me. "This is how you do it, Patty. You want to use the best gin around. That's Bombay Sapphire—expensive, but well worth the price. And you use some dry vermouth. Five-to-one ratio, gin to vermouth, or you're just playing around. You mix it with a lot of ice—you got a martini that isn't freezing cold, you got nothing." He shakes the mixture briskly, then pours it into two glasses, adds two olives to each one. He slides my drink in front of me, takes a generous sip of his own. Then he puts his glass down carefully, spreads his fingers apart, lifts his lips away from his teeth, and sucks in air. "Yes, indeed," he says.

I taste mine, stop just short of gasping. "Wow!"

"Goddamn right." He takes another generous swallow.

"Wow," I say, again.

"Very *close* now," Muriel yells down.

"We're coming!" Artie yells back, but we don't move. Frank is onto "Summer Wind." I am onto watching Artie at Home, a new person. This is not the man who sat quietly sweating in the backseat of my car.

I take another sip. And notice something. "Hey, Artie," I say. "The stems on these glasses are naked *wom*en!"

He flushes. "Got 'em when I was in the army, stationed in Korea. I'm sorry if they offend you."

"No, it's . . ." I'm really not offended. I think probably Artie is grandfathered in for this sort of thing. I look at the glasses more closely. "But I'll tell you one thing, Artie. Nobody has boobs like this." The breasts on the woman tip up impossibly. Impossibly.

"Know what I used to say about these glasses? I used to say, 'Listen, you're a very important guest. For you, I'm going to use my breast glasses.' "

"Very funny," I say. Then, looking again at the mesmerizing anatomy of the stem woman, "Is this what guys really like? Seriously."

"Artie!" we hear.

"One MINUTE!"

"No, NOW, the gravy's DONE! I want to get everything on the TAble!"

"Will you for Christ's sake *wait* a minute, Muriel! I haven't even told her yet!"

A moment, and then Muriel starts down the basement steps, stops halfway. She has a sheer white apron tied around her waist, a dishtowel in her hands. "So tell her." Her voice is quiet, simple sounding.

He looks at me, bites at a corner of his lip, then turns away.

Muriel comes down the rest of the way.

"Artie?" I say.

"Yeah." He keeps his back to me, starts putting things away.

"You want *I* should tell her?" Muriel asks.

"Tell me what?" I say, giggling a little. Then, holding up my glass, "Bartender? May I have another?"

Muriel sits beside me, folds her dishcloth into a neat rectangle, lays it on the bar. "I wouldn't mind a martini myself, Arthur."

"You can't drink on your medication."

"Neither can you."

"I have a joint," I say.

They both look at me.

"Did you ever try it?"

"Are you talking about marijuana?" Muriel says.

"Of course she's talking about marijuana," Artie says. And then, to me, "Are you talking about marijuana?"

"Yes."

"You smoke marijuana?"

"Well . . . hardly ever. Really. But I do have a joint that somebody gave me." Mark, actually, on one of the dates we had. We went to the zoo and got stoned.

"Well, I'd like to try it," Artie says.

"Oh, my God."

"I would, Muriel. What the hell. We always wondered what it was like."

"I'll get it," I say. "It's in my purse."

"Oy, she carries dope in her purse," Muriel says. "Our real estate agent is a dope addict. Who drives us around in her *car.* We could have been killed! We could have gotten *bust*ed!"

"I'm not a dope addict!" I say, at the same time that Artie says, "Muriel! She's a nice girl! You love Patty!"

"Well," she sniffs. "I used to."

"You know, Muriel," I say, "it's no big deal. It's kind of like your martinis for our age."

"I hardly think so."

"It is, but it's less dangerous."

"Ha! That's what they tell you. The next thing you know—*smack*."

"Oh, that's not true," I say. "It's just something I do every now and then for fun."

"Go get it," Artie says. And then, to Muriel, "Come on. I want you should try it with me."

Muriel's hands are folded in her apron. She looks down at them, then back up at me. "Turn off the flame on the gravy when you go up, would you? Does this take long?"

"Not long at all," I promise.

When I come back down, I open my wallet and take the flattened joint out. "Oh my God, look at that," Muriel says. "Is that a rubber you have in there, too?!"

I look up, embarrassed.

"Muriel," Artie says.

"Never mind, that's exactly what it is."

He gives her a look.

"Fine," she says, looking away and busying herself with the curls at the nape of her neck.

I squeeze the joint back into shape, put it to my lips, and look at Artie, Bacall. He reaches into his pocket, pulls out his pipe lighter, and puts the flame to the joint, Bogart. I take a hit, then hand the joint to him. "Hold it in," I say in the pinched voice of the participant.

"Yeah, I know."

"How do you know?" Muriel asks.

"I'm sure he's seen it a million times," I answer for him.

Artie inhales, passes the joint to Muriel. She hesitates, holding the thing like it's fifty times bigger than it is. Then she squeezes her eyes shut and inhales deeply. She coughs spectacularly, opens her eyes, and says, "That's it. No more," and passes the joint to me.

"I really can't believe we're doing this," I say.

"*You* can't," Muriel says. "Imagine if our grandchildren could see us! Artie, can you imagine? Can you imagine what little Howard would say?"

"Well, everything's changed." Artie turns around to take the needle off the record, which ended some time ago. Then he turns back to me, shrugs. "I got cancer. Terminal."

I feel instantly sober. I look at the joint in my hand, ridiculous now, low; and put it out. "Oh, Artie." I have no idea what to say next. What I feel is a peculiar sense of sad and frustrated privilege: I'm honored that they are sharing this with me; I feel obliged to do something about it; and I know I can't. I look at Muriel, at her soft, crushed face, and get off my stool to hug her. Then I lean over the bar to hug Artie.

"All right," he says, patting my back. "Okay."

"Maybe I could just have a *little* martini," Muriel says.

He leans over the bar, kisses her forehead. "You got it, my beautiful girl." We are all tearful and we are all pretending that we are not.

"You wouldn't know it to look at her now," he tells me, "but she was some hot tomato." He puts an inch of drink into a glass, hands it to her.

"I'm telling you," Muriel says, agreeing with him. And holds her glass up to him for a long, silent toast.

A little while later, in the overly articulated speech of the moderately drunk person, Muriel says, "I told him, what the hell do I want that cottage for, Artie? I got everything. I was only playing around with the real estate thing." She leans in close to me, blinks. "I'm sorry. I guess we wasted an awful lot of your time."

"I didn't mind a bit."

"I still think we should get it," Artie says. "One of us might as well have our dream spot."

"I *got* what I want," she says. "And that's all. I know my own mind. You think I don't know my own mind?"

I smell something burning. "Muriel?" I say, sniffing.

"Oh, Jesus." She stands up, then stops, holds her forehead. "Uh-oh. I guess I'm a little dizzy."

"I'll go," Artie says.

I follow his zigzag progress up the steps, then watch as he uncovers the ruined dinner.

We hear Muriel come slowly up the stairs, and then she is standing with us, looking into the pot. "But I *planned* this," is all she says.

After tuna sandwiches and sliced tomatoes and frozen yogurt, Artie walks me out to my car. "You're sure you're all right to drive?" he asks.

"I'm fine. Are you all right? And Muriel?"

"Don't worry. We had a good time."

"I'm glad you decided against the cottage. I think you have a lovely place right here."

"Yeah. But maybe we'll still come and look sometimes, huh?"

"I'd like that."

"Okay, kid."

"I really would, Artie."

"Listen, Patty, Muriel wanted to give you a tip. For . . . you know, all you've done. But I thought it might insult you. I guess I think of us as friends. I hope I wasn't wrong."

"Well . . . how much of a tip?" I say. We smile. And then I kiss his cheek and get in the car.

On the drive back, I think, maybe this isn't so sad. They got to have their lives together. She will be with him ferociously until the end. That's not so bad, considering.

At home, there is a message on my machine from Elaine to call her. I sit down with my coat still on, dial her number.

"Artie Berkenheimer has cancer," I tell her.

"Oh no, really?"

"Yeah. But they're . . . all right. They're just carrying on as usual, you know—she kvetches, he kvetches back. We got stoned together."

"Who?"

"Me and the Berkenheimers."

"Are you serious?"

"Yeah."

"You got *stoned* with the Berkenheimers?"

"Yeah!"

"It sounds like a contradiction in terms."

I laugh, slide my coat off. "I know."

"Hold on a second," Elaine says, and covers the mouthpiece of the phone. "It's Patty," I hear her say. Then something else I can't understand. And then, to me, "Listen, I need to ask you something."

"Who's over there?"

"Well, that's what I need to ask you. Sort of."

"Is it Mark?"

"Yeah."

"I don't care, Elaine."

"Don't you?"

"No, I told you. He's not right for me."

"So . . . if we . . ."

"If you want to fuck him, Elaine, then fuck him. I don't care."

"See? You're pissed. You do care."

"No I *don't* care. I don't care if you sleep with him, I don't care if you marry him! I just don't like this whole . . . set-up thing. I don't like that the two of you are over there talking about me. Just do what you want, it's not up to me. I don't have anything to do with Mark anymore."

Silence.

"What?" I say.

"You're pissed, Patty, why can't you just say it?"

"All right, Elaine, I'm pissed, but it's not because of *Mark*!"

"What's it because of?"

"It's because of *you,* all right? It's because of you."

"But what did I *do*? I apologized a million times to you for—"

"I told you, I don't *care* about Mark. You're welcome to him."

Silence, again.

And then I say, "Look, we'll talk about it another time. I'm tired, now. I want to go to bed."

"Yeah, all right. Me, too."

"Right. As you indicated."

I hang up pretty hard. The receiver falls off the phone, and I put it back on, then take it off again. I don't want anybody to call me for anything. I want to be alone. And I am. And Elaine is not. And I guess that's what I'm angry about. It's not that she has Mark. It's that she has *somebody.* As she always does. As she *always* does, there is never a doubt. I would like to have her privileges, for just a day. Just for one day, I'd like all the favors she is granted because of her goddamn looks to be handed to me. Jesus, it's a wonder she doesn't suffocate.

I wash up for bed, then put the phone back on the hook. And then pick it up again, to be sure the dial tone's there, so someone can call. Sometimes I'm a liar. But sometimes the truth is just too tiresome to bear.

9

Elaine and I are at our favorite Mexican restaurant, on our third margarita. "Well, that's it, I can't even see straight," Elaine says. "We're going to have to take a cab home."

"I know." As for me, I can no longer feel the roof of my mouth.

"I hope I don't puke," she says. "I get carsick in backseats."

"I saw a movie where she puked in her purse."

"That's no better. That's worse!"

I consider this. True. "Well, if you do puke in the cab, wait till after I get out. I know all the drivers."

"So do I!"

"Yeah, but the cabdriver won't be mad if it's you. He'll think it's cute."

Elaine puts her glass down, settles back in her chair. "Okay, fine. Let's talk about it."

"What?"

"I've been sitting here all night waiting for you to bring it up."

"Bring what up?"

"Your jealousy."

It occurs to me to deny it. But I don't.

"What am I supposed to do, Patty? What will make you not so mad at me? I see it all the time. When we go into the ladies' room and we're putting our lipstick on, I feel you watching me and I . . . I feel this *rage* coming from you."

"It's not *rage,* Elaine." Yes it is. That's exactly what it is. I hate that it's in me. But it is.

"Well, what is it, then?"

I shrug, lick some salt off my glass, find a very interesting spot on the tablecloth.

Our waiter glides up to our table like a swan. "How's everything here?" he asks, smiling at Elaine. She doesn't answer. Nor do I.

"Ladies?"

"I want to ask you something," I say. "Do you guys watch people, and wait until they're obviously involved in an important conversation, and then come flying over to ask about the chimichangas?"

"You didn't get chimichangas."

"We need some privacy," Elaine says quietly.

"Fine." He lays the check on the table. "Whenever you're ready." He spins smartly on one heel, starts to walk away.

"Excuse me?" I say.

He turns back, wary.

"I'm sorry. It's her I'm mad at. Because I'm jealous of her."

"Okay," he says.

"It feels kind of good to just say it."

"Yeah. I'll bet it does."

"Patty," Elaine says.

"Could we have another drink?" I ask. I don't really want one. I just thought it might be nice to order more.

"Sure."

I hold up the check. "I think you'll need this."

"On the house."

After he leaves, Elaine says, "I just want to say something. I'm sick of talking about relationships and problems. I'm sick of everyone being in therapy, overanalyzing everything to death. Sometimes a cigar is just a cigar, you know? Well, okay, maybe not a cigar. But let's just say everything's fine between you and me. Okay? Mostly, it is."

"True. That's true." I take in a breath. "So. How's Mark?"

She sits up, looks straight at me. "I love him. All right?" She picks up the new margarita the waiter has set before her, holds it up to me.

I clink glasses with her. "Well!"

"I guess that doesn't tell you how he is, though."

"Do you think . . . you might get married?"

"I think we might."

"Okay, I have to ask you something."

"What?"

"Please don't make the bridesmaids' dresses have big bows at the waist. Or be pastel lace."

"You mean like at Linda Beauman's wedding, where all the bridesmaids looked like gigantic after-dinner mints?"

"Yes."

"Do you think I would do that to you?"

"No. But if I ever get married, I'm going to do it to you."

"If you ever get married, I'll wear a Hefty garbage bag if you want."

"Maybe you shouldn't be so decent, Elaine."

"Maybe I'm not always."

"I want to know something. Is he good in bed?"

She sighs. "Well, first I loved him. So it's different."

"Come on, Elaine."

She smiles, nods.

"I'm happy for you," I say. And I am. I also feel a roaring inside my chest, doing all it can to stay there and not come out of my mouth.

When I was in high school, I hung out with a big bunch of girls, there were nine of us. Every morning, we went to the girls' bathroom so we could smoke. We would sit on the floor and everyone had to step over us. It was very satisfying; I have yet to feel such a strong sense of righteous belonging. One day we were talking about marriage. "Patty will be first, that's for sure," Trudy Oldsman said, blowing a perfect smoke ring my way. "No I won't!" I said. "Uh-*huh*!" they all chorused back. And really, I secretly thought so, too.

After I get home, I call Elaine. "Are you sick?" I ask.

"No. I just have to keep holding onto the wall so the room stays still."

"Elaine, I want to tell you something. I am jealous of you."

"I know. It's all right."

"You know, I've never gotten to be first. All my life, every time I've tried for something, I might come close, but I never win. I think the precedent was set when I was nine, when I got second prize on Captain Cody's show for 'Guess the Silhouette.' It was a hot dog, I knew right away, and I called and was told I was the winner, but then the person on the line said, 'Oh, wait a minute.' And then it turned out someone else was first. Hey, that wasn't you, Elaine, was it? Did you win that hot-dog silhouette contest?"

"No, thank God, or you might never speak to me again."

"Well, I was Ms. Runner-up."

"Runner-up isn't so bad."

"It is when that's what you always are. And when your best friend is always the winner. But . . . I've been lying here thinking, and that's not what's really wrong. It's not you I'm mad at. It's me. You know? I'm mad at me."

"For what?"

"For . . . I don't know. For missing the boat. For running out of time."

"You're not out of time."

"Well . . ."

"You're not!"

"Oh, Elaine. You know when you're taking a plane in the middle of the afternoon, and you wake up that day and you can't really do anything and so you end up leaving for the airport early?"

"Yeah."

"That's what I feel like."

"Patty, if you could just—"

"I know what you're going to say. About Ethan, right? But I can't. I can't stop loving him. And I just don't think I can tell you why."

"Try."

"He's . . . I just find him so . . . beautiful, and so easy to be with.

I love his sense of humor. I feel a kind of safety with him that I never . . . Oh, what's the use? How can I explain it to you? Sometimes the difference between what I feel and what I want to say is so vast. It makes me think the invention of language was only a step backward."

"It's just that you *keep* yourself from so much by loving him," Elaine says. "Maybe you don't want a relationship, really. Did that ever occur to you?"

"I do want a relationship!"

"Well . . . think about that the next time you waste a weekend with Ethan."

I turn on my back, sigh.

After I hang up the phone, I go into the kitchen for a drink of water, stare out at the moonlit backyard. I think about how I used to like playing "Truth or Dare," but only for the truth part of it. I wished, in fact, that the game could simply *be* "Truth," and that you would play it by going into a small closet with your partner. You would close the door to absent yourself from the usual world and sit in velvety darkness, necessarily close to a person who would put their lips to your ear to whisper something absolutely real to you. Something primal. Whenever I imagined this, I could feel the movement of air coming from the person's mouth into my ear. I could feel the warmth in it, and the damp. I could smell earth and sun. I could feel the small hairs on the back of my neck rise up from the relief of hearing one small thing at last spoken so truly it made my insides feel righted.

When we played "Truth or Dare," I chose truth every time, but the questions and answers were only those calculated to embarrass one person and thrill the others. That kind of truth was not what I was interested in. That was not at all what I wanted to know. But what could I say? How could I ask? I was never in a closet, in the dark, the lies of my eyes obliterated and the moment for revelation finally at hand.

I've told a few other people this story, and they either got uncomfortable or said, "Oh, uh-huh." But when I told Ethan, his eyes filled with tears. "I know," he said, and held me for a long time. I took that moment for what I wanted it to be: an acknowledgment that he too ached for that kind of intimacy, and I was the one to give it to him. I was as helpless as an addict before he can even think of changing: stuck in overwhelming want, governed by bone-deep need. Oh, that bad pleasure—it's amazingly good.

The next morning, someone in the office tells me there's a call for me on line three. "Patty Murphy," I say into the phone—quietly, out of respect for my hangover. I'm hoping someone will say, "I want to buy a very big house. You don't have to do anything." The last rental I did will barely bring me enough to buy a bag of groceries. But if the Flanagans decide on the high-priced condo I've shown them four times now, I'll be all right for a while. I like the Flanagans. They've been married for six years but they're still wildly in love. They look like brother and sister: both black-haired, blue-eyed people. Maybe a kind of narcissism is a good thing in a relationship.

The voice I hear at the other end of the phone says, "I want to buy your most expensive property. I'll pay cash and there's a good tip in it for you, too," but it doesn't count—it's only my brother, Johnny.

"Hey, come sign the papers," I say. "I'm about to starve."

In the background, I hear the sounds coming from the garage Johnny owns. "Intensive Car," he calls it. There are metal parts banging together, the low sound of men's voices, country and western on the radio, of course—Johnny lives in Nashville. He married a gorgeous redhead who used to be on *Hee-Haw* and now sings in the clubs around town. I like her, Nancy's her name, although she pronounces it "Ninecy." They already have three kids, all boys, all with little baby southern accents. "Aint Patty," they call me. I wonder if this time they'll get a sister.

"Listen," Johnny says now. "What's up with Mom?"

"What do you mean?"

"I don't know; she sounded strange last time I talked to her. Kind of distant."

"Oh, she's just mad at me. Her wrath makes her preoccupied. It's her hobby lately, like needlepoint."

"Why is she mad at you?"

"Because I stopped seeing someone she thought I should marry."

"Is that right?"

"That's right, and don't you go getting on the bandwagon with her."

"Hey, I just want you to be happy."

"I know."

"But Dad says Mom is—"

"I check on them, Johnny. You know I'd tell you if anything was up."

"It's just hard being this far away, you know? She really didn't sound like herself."

"Well, she's getting older. You change."

"Yeah. Maybe. Maybe that's all it is."

"I'll go see them this weekend. I'll call you and let you know how they are."

After I hang up the phone, I lean back in my swivel chair, clasp my hands behind my head. I hate being the oldest. I hate being the only one who stayed, the one responsible for my parents while my sisters and brother do whatever they want. I hate being the only one unmarried and childless, the one with zero prospects, the one they all worry about in ways that are just a little too self-satisfied, the one who is the unspoken agenda at Thanksgiving, at Christmas, at any other significant family gathering. I need something. Right now, I just need something. I wish someone would walk in the office and hand me a bouquet. Or a cheeseburger. Anything. I shoot a rubber band across the room, hit Melanie Olson in the back of the head. There.

"Hey!" she says, turning around.

"Sorry."

"What's the matter, you need a break?"

"Yeah."

"Take off. I'll do the phones."

I open my desk drawer, take out my purse.

"Patty?"

"Yeah?"

"Bring me back a cheeseburger?"

"Sure." My fantasy. That someone else gets to have. Story of my life, as they say. I might as well bring her back a little bouquet, too. You can get a nice mix for a few dollars over at Quick Mart. I'll bring her purples and pinks; I like purples and pinks.

10

Sometimes, not often, it happens that I can't sleep. It's worst when I've already been asleep for a little while, and then suddenly get jerked into hyperawareness. It's the opposite of a natural awakening, when you open your eyes rested and calm and perfectly willing to give the world another go. This is more like a hand reaching into your center to squeeze it. And then squeeze it again, harder.

I look at the clocks. One-ten, they agree. Fine. That's not so bad. I can pretend I've been out to a party and have just gotten into bed. And as long as I'm pretending, I will say that I had quite a wonderful time. Yes, I did. I said many good and clever things. People were thinking, Oh, thank goodness someone like *her* came. What did she say her name was? And she said she was *single*?

No. I am not believing myself. My hand is not holding a drink and some clever canapé. It is lying all by itself against my stomach, which is dressed in stained flannel pajamas.

I sit up, notice a dime-sized area of headache in each temple. I can feel sleep scratching against the insides of my eyelids, but I know it will be a long time before I can relax back into it. I look at the clock again. 1:11. It is so dark. I feel my hands clench into fists. I feel my breathing start to quicken.

Here we go.

Nothing will help this, I know. Not the sight of a calm container of cottage cheese in my refrigerator, not some late-night movie, not even a phone call to the Samaritans, which I am ashamed to say I actually tried once. I said right away that I was not really suicidal, but I still felt guilty, hogging a phone line when someone might be standing on a bridge, trying to get through on their cellular phone—which was yet another thing that did not bring the person happiness. Anyway, the highly trained volunteer didn't believe I was only anxious. She spoke to me so tenderly she made me sob. She got me in touch with a deep kind of grief that made me think maybe I *was* suicidal. All in all, not a particularly helpful experience.

I get up, go into the living room, turn on all the lights. It is so quiet I swear I can hear the disturbance in the air every time I move. The darkness does not dissipate, but only seems pushed up into the corners of the room, where it hangs, vulturelike. I sit on the sofa, pull my knees up to my chest, rest my chin on them. Sniff. Think: I am thirty-six years old and no one knows me, not one person, not really. Not my family. Not Elaine. Not Ethan. My mind catches on this last one. Because Elaine may not know the realest, deepest me, but Ethan does. There has always been a kind of holding back in me from Elaine. I can't help this particular smallness of heart; find me one woman who doesn't withhold just a bit from another woman who looks like that. But Ethan really does know me. I can be all of my selves with him. I wore an emerald-green evening gown with him on a night I spent fifteen minutes just getting my lipstick on, and I can tell you that that night I looked as good as I ever will and felt it, too, I felt beautiful. I have also sat on the sofa with Ethan wearing a sweat outfit and a robe and mismatched socks, watching *Blazing Saddles* for the ninth (9th) time. I wore adult-formula Clearasil smeared across my entire forehead that time too, then sabotaged my efforts by stuffing myself with Cape Cod potato chips dipped in Lipton's famous recipe for insti–weight gain.

I pick up the phone. He is the one I can call, he is always the one. His phone rings once, twice, part of a third time. And then there is his sleepy "Hello?"

"Ethan?"

"Patty. What happened?"

"Nothing. I can't sleep. I feel anxious as hell."

"Tell me."

"I don't know. I don't know."

"Death?"

"No."

"Did you say something bad to someone important?"

"No. It's . . . Here. Here's what it is. I fell asleep the other night, and I woke up the next morning and went to the bathroom and I saw myself in the mirror and I still had red lipstick on from the day before and no one had even seen it."

"Oh. Yeah." He yawns noisily. "I feel like that sometimes when I clean the house really well and then a week goes by and no one even comes over. Nobody sees any of the casual arrangements of stuff I left lying around to try to impress them. So I clean it all over again. I feel like Sisyphus in an apron."

"It's more than that, Ethan. It's that I think, oh God, I'm going to be a woman sitting all by herself forever. It's not going to happen to me; I won't ever get to have a family. I will be in this painful part of life for a while and then I will be too old to have children and then I will be a spinster—oh, yes, people still think that way, yes they do!—and then I will start slowly getting ridiculous and then I will die alone and they will find me because of the smell. Oh God, Ethan, think of it, it will just be so embarrassing."

"You know, Patty—"

"No. I know what you're going to say. You're going to say that all my thoughts are black like this because I need to go to sleep. You're going to say that it will all look different in the morning. But it's not true."

"I wasn't going to say that."

"What were you going to say?"

I hear some muffled movement. I'll bet he's turning from his side onto his back. I'll bet he smells good, like sleep and the muted leftovers of his exotically earthy cologne. I'll bet his sheets are beautiful. Well, I know his sheets are beautiful, they always are, he orders them from a catalog for people with good taste. And a fair amount of money.

He sighs. "I was going to say . . . I was going to say I think about that too, I have that same fantasy. I just don't think I'm going to meet him. Ever. I'm ready to give up."

I hold very still.

"Patty?"

I make my voice get as calm and reasonable as I can, difficult to do with a heart rate of about 150 and a longing so strong it steals breathing space. "Ethan, don't you see that there is a very good thing to do about this?"

"What?"

"Why don't you just get me pregnant? It would give us such a good reason to live. It would leave something of us behind, it would matter more that we were here, it would."

Silence. I take another step on this thinnest of ice.

"I know how you feel about children. Remember when we were sitting in the park by the playground that day and that little tow-headed boy came over and just stood in front of you for so long? I saw what happened inside you; I know that feeling, I *know* it. You should have seen your face, Ethan. This . . . softness. This light. In your head, you were tucking him in, laying his little cowboy robe at the foot of his bed, you were pushing his hair aside to kiss his little soapy-smelling forehead. You were doing something like that, weren't you? Weren't you?"

He sighs. "Digging worms."

"What?"

"Digging worms, we were digging worms because I was taking him fishing. And I was going to teach him not to be afraid of worms because I am."

"Right. See? Right." I close my eyes, lean forward, huddle over the phone and speak into it as though it were my confessor: quietly, plaintively; and with an equal mix of truth and shame and hope. "Listen, Ethan. Your need to have children is every bit as strong as mine. Do you think an opportunity is just lying there, drumming its fingers, waiting for you to say yes? You think you can just grab some woman when you're ready and say, 'Hey, I've got an idea'? Something will be so wasted in both of us if we don't have children. I really believe we'll miss it all our lives. And who should *be* the mother of your child, Ethan? Who, if not me?" I take a deep breath, feel my toes curling inside my slippers. Well. So much for the even-handed delivery I'd had in mind. He probably hung up half an hour ago. "Ethan?"

"Where are you?"

"Home!"

"No. In your cycle."

"Menstrual?"

"Yeah."

"What do you mean? What if I were in the middle? What if I were ovulating?"

"Then . . . I'd come over."

"You would? You mean—?"

"Yes."

"This is *it*?, you'll have a *ba*by with me?"

"Yes."

"This is all the discussion we'll have to have, we'll just *do* it?"

"Don't you think you should lower your voice just a bit?"

"Am I yelling?"

"Yes."

"But this is—"

"Patty, I don't think there's anything to talk about, really. What do you want to do, decide now if he or she should play with guns? You're right. We know each other. We don't need . . . We *know* each other. We'll just take it as it happens. We'll work everything out. The main thing is, we'll have a child. We'll just do it. When you're . . . you know, ready."

"Ethan, I swear to God, I am exactly in the middle of my cycle. I've got an egg barreling down the pike, right in the strike zone, and it is a good egg. So to speak." Naturally I have no idea if this is true or not. But I will be very, very good from now on. I'll put a huge X on the calendar on the day I start. I'll take my temperature every day. Everything.

"I'll be there in twenty minutes."

"Okay. Okay. God! Ethan?"

"Yeah."

"I'll understand if we can't . . . if we have to, you know, use a turkey baster. Maybe you should bring a magazine. Also a turkey baster."

"Let's see what happens."

"Okay."

I put the phone back in the cradle. I see that I am on my knees, my knuckles pressed into my mouth. No one has ever felt such a mix of so much.

"You . . . changed?" Ethan asks, when I open the door.

I look down at my black dinner dress. "This, you mean?"

He comes in, hangs up his coat.

"I assume you don't ordinarily sleep in a dress. It's a nice dress, by the way. Very flattering."

"Thank you. I just . . . well . . . under the circumstances. I also, you know . . . took a bath. A little."

He leans in, sniffs me. "Nice."

"Thank you."

"Are you nervous, Patty?"

"Me? No! No! Are you?"

"No!"

"Okay. So before we . . . do you want anything? You know. Drink? Something?"

"No thanks. But you, uh . . . you go ahead. If you want. A drink. I don't mind. Well, of course I don't mind, why would I mind?"

I open the refrigerator. "I have some leftover spaghetti."

"Patty."

"Yeah?"

"It's two o'clock in the morning."

"Yeah. Yeah. So . . . cocoa?"

He sighs. "Come here."

"Okay."

I don't move.

"Let's just go lie down, all right? We'll just . . . lie down. Next to each other. We'll lie down first. And then . . . you know, we could talk."

"Right. That's good. Ethan?"

"Yeah."

"I . . . *am,* you know, just a *bit*—"

"Me, too. I'm scared shitless."

"I don't know why!"

"Me either."

"Well, I kind of know why."

"Me, too."

He crosses over to me, gently embraces me. I laugh. The sound is reminiscent of a braying donkey. I push away from him, step out of my heels, get a paper towel, and rub the lipstick from my mouth. "That's better," I say. And he kisses me. And I can feel each of us begin to relax into the other. I take his hand and lead him into the bedroom, where I have a single candle burning on the dresser.

"Oh, this is nice," he says, stretching out on the bed.

"I guess you're supposed to have fifty or sixty, all lit."

"Fire hazard," Ethan says. His eyes are closed. "Anyway, you get plenty of light from that one, it's a good-sized candle."

"So . . . I'm just going to get undressed," I say.

He opens his eyes. I pull my dress over my head, stand before him in my new underwear which thank God I bought just last week. It's a matching set. Black. Ethan doesn't move. "I thought I might as well get it over with," I say. "You don't have to get undressed yet, though."

"No, I will. I will." He stands up, unbuckles his belt, steps out of his pants.

"Do you want me to hang those up?"

"Well, I did just get them."

"Yeah, I thought they were new. Are they green? Or gray?"

"Greenish gray, I'd say." He hands them to me. They are so light, but warm.

"Are these silk?"

"Silk and wool. Sixty-forty. Zegna. Do you like them?"

I nod. My throat is dry. His legs are so nice.

"I thought . . . you know, yeah, I liked them, too. So, uh . . . I bought them! Obviously." He smiles, pushes his hair back. He is a movie, *Beautiful Man Undressing.* Next comes his sweater. A cream color, softness itself, Mongolian cashmere, sure as my knees are becoming unreliable. And now here is his shirt, smelling faintly of him. "Barbera," he says, gesturing at it with his chin. His arms are crossed over his chest. He looks like an inductee at an army recruitment center, except that his socks are too beautiful.

"Pardon me?" I say.

"Luciano Barbera. The shirt."

"Oh! Well, it's very nice."

"I spend way too much money on clothes."

"Yes, you do."

"I know."

I stand still, looking at him.

"So! I guess I'll just get under the covers," he says.

"Do you have an erection?"

"Jesus, Patty!"

"Well, I'm sorry. It's just that . . . I was . . . you know, wondering."

"Fine."

"Well, do you?"

". . . *Yes,* okay? Kind of. Keep talking, though, I'm sure we can get rid of it."

"I'm sorry. I'm sorry. I'll just hang these up."

I come back to the bed, slide in, remove my underwear, toss it overboard. As does Ethan. Then he reaches over and takes my hand, lies back, and closes his eyes.

"Nothing may happen this first time," he says. "It doesn't mean *any*thing if nothing happens. Against you. Well, against either of us, really."

"Okay."

I close my eyes, listen to the sound of us breathing.

"I just got this image," Ethan says. His voice is lazy; relaxed, now.

"Of what?"

"Of my father. Huh. I don't know why. I just all of a sudden saw him standing there."

I open my eyes, look over at him. "You never talk about him."

"I know." He keeps his eyes closed.

"How come?"

"Oh. . . . He was . . . impossible. Impossible. You couldn't love him. Well, you *did* love him, you couldn't help it, but he didn't want you to."

"Why not?"

Ethan opens his eyes. "It's not so uncommon. You don't know about this stuff, you come from such a normal family. Although they're so normal they're abnormal."

"I know; I'm lucky."

"I love your mother. And your father."

"They love you, too."

"I was so nervous the first time I met them. And your father was so . . . I mean, wearing that chef's hat, waving his king-size spatula over the grill, singing 'Shangri-La.' "

I smile, remembering.

"Patty?"

"Yeah."

Nothing.

". . . Ethan?"

He rises up on one elbow, pulls the covers down from my breasts, regards them.

I wait a nervous moment, then start to pull the covers back up. "Don't," he says. And then touches me as only, only, only he can. And what happens next, and next, is similar to how you never forget how to ride a bicycle. Let me say only this: he is on me here, and here, and here, Ethan is, Ethan; and I am on him; and then he is in me, moving, moving, moving, and I hear myself talking—just low, just a little—until there is no more talking and no more moving, nothing but the sense of peace that comes from something like seeing a wide green field, quiet.

"You know," I say, after a while, "no one would know you're gay."

"What's that supposed to be, a compliment?"

"Well, *yeah*. I guess. I'm sorry."

He kisses my forehead, then lies back against his pillow, sighs. "There's so much you just don't understand. That you *won't* understand."

I pick at a tuft on my bedspread. "I know." And then, "God, Ethan, we did it."

He turns to look at me. "Do you think there's any way you're . . . ? Do you think we might have really started a baby?"

I think about this, feel a sense of wonder as an answer. Then, "Yeah," I say. "I think we might have. We might have. Why? Are you sorry?"

"I'm not sorry. You know that I love you, Patty."

"You're supposed to say that be*fore,* so I'll do it."

"I do love you."

"I know, Ethan. I love you, too."

"I thought we should say that."

"Yes. I'm glad we did."

"Okay."

"Should we sleep for a while? And then I'll make you pancakes?"

"Yes."

"Okay. Ethan?"

"Yeah."

"I just want to say . . . I just want to tell you that this is enough. I know what this is, I do. And it's enough."

He falls asleep first. And I watch him for a long time. Afraid, in a way, to move.

"Why are your pancakes so good?" Ethan asks, as he runs water over his plate. A nearly unnecessary act; there's nothing left on it.

"First of all," I say, "you have to know when to stop mixing. And you have to put vanilla in. And you cook them in a lot of butter and throw the first batch away because they're disgusting."

"Too much to remember." He looks at his watch. "I've got to go. I'll call you later."

I have a very strange *Father-Knows-Best* Feeling: Ethan, kissing me on the cheek before he leaves for work, the smell of coffee and maple syrup on his breath from the breakfast I made him. I'll just finish the dishes, and then I'll finish growing the baby.

Ethan closes the door behind him, then opens it again. "Patty?"

"Yes?"

"I don't think we should tell anyone about this yet."

I say nothing, don't move.

"It's not because I'm having doubts or anything. I just . . . would like us to have it to ourselves for a while."

I nod. I'm not sure what to make of this.

"For Christ's sake, Patty, it's ro*man*tic!"

"Oh! All right. I won't tell anyone. I'm happy, though."

"We'll just wait and see, all right? We'll wait and see if you are before we tell. And if you are, you can't eat rare meat."

"Why?"

"Something about a disease you can catch. A guy at work, his wife is pregnant, and she was told not to eat rare meat. Or to clean the cat's litter box."

"I don't have a cat."

Ethan's face changes.

"Oh," I say. "I'm sorry."

"It's okay."

"Do you want to get another one?"

"No, not yet. Not yet."

"Well. Maybe you'll have . . . you know. Something else."

"You don't have to keep it a secret from *us,* Patty. We can say it. Maybe I'll have a baby. Maybe we will."

"Yes."

"God!"

"I know." I smile, tighten the belt on my bathrobe, full of what I might call pride.

"Walk me out to the car," Ethan says.

I put on my coat, go out with him. The day is clear, beautiful. A good sign.

Ethan starts the engine, rolls down the window. "I'll see you." He looks shy; I want to touch his face. Instead, I wave good-bye.

On the way back into the house, I see Sophia coming down her steps. She's after the morning paper. I pick it up, bring it to her.

She stares after Ethan's car. "He is sleeping here now in the night?"

"Well, we're trying to get me pregnant," I say. And then, "Oh, Jesus."

Sophia's eyes widen. "This is for true?"

"I wasn't supposed to tell."

Sophia draws an *X* over her heart.

"I can't believe it! It just popped out!"

"Well, some excitement, it can't wait."

"Please don't tell him I told you."

"We never speak! If I speak on Ethan, maybe I'm faint. Whew!"

I look down, smile. "Yeah."

"You want to know?" Sophia asks.

"What?"

"You want to know if you have pregnant?"

"Well, I . . . It was just last night, you know. I'll wait a couple weeks."

"I can tell now."

"You can?"

She nods gravely.

"Okay. So . . . am I?"

"No, you must come in. Lie down. I have to see your belly. And some . . . twine? I need some twine and one some thing from you and from Ethan."

"I have a sock."

"Yes. Good. Bring it, two socks, one from you, too. And I can tell you. Many times, I have done this. Guess how many times I am wrong."

"None."

"That is it. You have a bingo."

I am lying on Sophia's nubby green sofa. It carries the faint smell of mothballs, which I hope does not cause birth defects. Lace curtains are pulled back from her window, and the light shines prettily through the blue glassware she has lined up there. Blue. Boy. It's a boy.

"It's a boy," I say.

Sophia opens her eyes and stops swinging the bundle of socks over my stomach.

"You got it so soon?"

"No. I'm just kidding. Guessing. You know, I saw blue, I thought 'boy.' "

She tsks, begins speaking rapidly, "*You* must only lie still, I telled you! If you, you're thinking, What is baby? What is baby? and *I* am thinking, What is ba—No! If I am thinking, *Is* baby? *Is* baby?, not *What* is baby?, is too confusing for answer to come!"

"Whoa. Pardon?"

Sophia leans down into my face. "Here is your part: nothing. Easy."

"Okay."

"Close your eyes."

I feel a tiny breeze, the movement of the prophetic sock bundle. It glides back and forth across my stomach. And then Sophia draws in a sharp breath.

"What?" I say. "What's wrong?"

She shakes her head solemnly.

"Oh God, I'm too old, aren't I, there's something wrong with it, isn't there?"

"No. What it is, you have the new life. Is there. Starting."

"Oh, Sophia." I start to laugh, sit up, close my robe. "You can't really tell."

"I have never wrong. I have never check so early, is true. But! I have never wrong."

"Well." I smile.

"So." She smiles back. I hear her clock chime the hour, as though something else in the house needs to mark the moment.

"I feel so . . . God!" I laugh loudly, then flush, embarrassed at my excessiveness. "I'm sorry, I guess I'm—"

"No! Not to feel shame. Is every time, a miracle. On every woman. You can be high up glad, is okay. Is right."

"Yes. It is right."

"You want now some tea?"

"No. Thank you, no."

"Later, you can help me with some few letters?"

"Sure."

"I have lately winned some microware."

"You did?"

She shrugs. "You help me fill out on some paper, I send it, and—pah!"

"You won some microwave dishes?"

"I show you." She shuffles out to her kitchen, opens her cupboard, and shows me neatly arranged white containers with glass lids.

"Wow. How did you do that?"

"You help me! I fill out form, is all."

"Huh!"

"You want, I can share."

"No, I don't need it. You keep it."

"Okay. I thank you some more." She bows her head, curtsies a little.

"You're very welcome. Thank *you*. For the . . . test."

"So, you knew anyway. You did. A woman can know, if she does want."

"Yeah. I think you're right."

"Today I make cabbage soup. And I save some for you. For you and you-know-who. Sweet and sour, is good to introduce on life."

11

Back in my house, I start a pot of coffee, dial Elaine's number. "What?" she says, on the second ring.

"Can you come over?"

"Patty. Jesus. Do you know what time it is?"

"No."

"Eight o'clock. Do you know what day it is?"

Do I ever.

"Saturday. Listen, I was up around six. I waited two hours to call you. Pretend it's a workday. If it were a workday, you'd be up already."

"The purpose of a Saturday is to have it *not* be a workday. And the purpose of it not being a workday is to have eight o'clock not matter. I think this makes sense. I'll hang up now and you think about it and in a few hours call back and tell me if I'm right."

"I'm pregnant."

Silence.

"Elaine?"

"By whom?"

"Well, actually, Ethan."

Another silence. A bigger one. Then, "My God, Patty, are you serious?"

"Yes."

"You're *preg*nant?"

"Yes. Perhaps yes. I could actually be pregnant."

"Well, are you or aren't you?"

"Okay, I haven't done the test. But that's just a technicality. I've done everything else."

"With *Ethan*?"

"Yeah. Ethan."

"I'm coming over. Wait right there. Don't go anywhere. Goddamn it. Make some coffee."

"It's made."

"And don't you DRINK any, either, if you're pregnant!" This last is yelled into the phone from somewhere across the room. She's getting dressed, I know. She flings her pajamas into the farthest corner of the room. Then she puts her socks on first. "You can't have coffee ANYMORE!"

"I had milk," I shout.

I hear her pick up the phone again, say impatiently, "What?"

"I had milk."

"That's disgusting. Here I come."

I was wrong; Elaine has no socks on when she comes in. Snow is caked along the edges of her sneakers. She is clutching her coat closed, shivering.

"Jesus, Elaine. It wasn't an emergency."

I take off my slippers, slide them across the room toward her.

She steps out of her shoes and little clumps of snow fall out like frosting. She puts on the slippers, pulls her coat tight around her, starts picking up the snow.

"Leave it," I say. Later, I'll scrub the floor. Happily. This happens when you get pregnant, you get very domestic. "Take off your coat."

"It won't be easy. I think it's frozen onto me."

"Why didn't you wear your boots?"

"I couldn't find them. Anyway, who cares about boots, tell me everything." She hangs her coat up, goes to the kitchen table to sit down. I give her a mug of coffee, then sit opposite her.

"Well?" she says, her blue eyes wide and beautiful, which, for the first time, does not get on my nerves in the slightest.

"Well," I say. "I just think we both realized—"

"No, no, no," she says. "Not in the abstract. Do it like, 'He came over and he was wearing yak yak yak and I hung up his coat and I was thinking yak yak yak and he walked up to me and carried me to the bed' . . . Like that."

"Well, he hardly carried me to the bed."

She shrugs unhappily. "I know. They never do."

"Well, why do we *want* them to?"

"I don't know. But we do. Don't we? I do."

"Why? It would just be embarrassing when they needed to buy a hernia belt later."

"Some time today, Patty, you'll probably tell me what happened."

"I know. I am. Okay, I called him last night because I couldn't sleep, I was all anxious and upset."

Elaine sits motionless for the whole story, and when I'm done she gets up and comes over and hugs me. Then, suddenly, she lets go. "Did I hurt you?"

"I'm *fine,*" I say. "It's just me, Elaine."

"No. You're different now."

"I'm not any different."

"Yes, you are."

"I know."

"Does it feel different?"

"Yes."

"How?"

"I don't know. Maybe . . . in my belly, low down in my belly. It feels softer. Like there's this liquid spot of . . . happening."

"Wow. Really?" She puts her hand to me, gently.

I start laughing. "I don't know. I think so. There's just something, I feel something."

Elaine puts her cup in the sink. "Get dressed. We have to go shopping."

"For what?"

"Maternity clothes. And those little baby OshKosh jeans. And . . . you know, a giraffe or something."

"Not yet!"

"Okay then, how about a pregnancy test?"

"Yeah. Okay. But I am, I just know it."

"We'll see."

"Fifty bucks," I say.

"Five."

We shake. And I am aware, as I never was before, that her hand used to be a baby's.

• • •

Late that evening, the phone rang.

"I told," Ethan says. "I'm sorry."

"Ethan!"

"I know, but I . . . it just slipped out. To Ed McCracken. He won't tell anyone, though. I don't know, it's like I had to say it to someone else."

"Well . . ."

"I'm sorry."

"It's okay. I told, too."

"Who?"

"Elaine."

"Oh, I knew you'd tell her. It's all right."

"And . . . Well, kind of Sophia, too."

"Why?"

"Well, the same thing as *you,* Ethan, it just slipped out! But she did this test? And I'm pregnant, she said. Plus Elaine and I bought a test from CVS, I'm going to wait ten days and then I'm going to do it."

"I'm coming for that."

"Yes, I thought so."

"Those you can believe."

"Yeah. Although . . . I believe Sophia." My voice is small saying this.

"Me, too." His voice is reverent.

"We bought some other things, too."

"What?"

"Oh . . . clothes. For . . . you know, both of us. Me and it. Him or her. And a few toys. And . . . just . . . a mobile." Actually, "we" did not buy all that. Elaine did. It's going to be pretty wonderful to have her live vicariously through me. Certainly it's going to save me some money. I'm glad she makes so much writing ad copy. "Oh, and one stuffed animal," I say, "one of those big chimps in the window at Kids And."

"Holding the banana?"

"Yeah! Have you seen it?"

"I bought it."

"Ethan!"

"Well, you did too!"

"I think we need to slow down."

"Listen, all I got is one chimp. You're acting like the buyer for Bloomingdale's."

"I'm going to do the test on Friday the third," I say.

"Friiiday the thirrrd," I hear him say under his breath and I know he is writing me down in his calendar. I feel a sudden sense of security, of pride, knowing I will be appearing on those calendar pages often, now.

"Do it at seven o'clock," Ethan says.

"Well, you're supposed to do it in the morning."

"I know, that's what I meant. Seven in the morning, then I can be there before I go to work. Don't forget, we need to get your first voided specimen."

"What?"

"The first pee of the day. That's when you have the most concentration of the hormone it looks for—hCG, it's called. Human chorionic gonadotrophin."

"How do *you* know all this?"

"I asked. Did you get the test where there's two in one?"

"Don't worry about it," I say. "We're all set." Did I get *the* test? That *one*? I go into the bathroom, look at the pregnancy tests all lined up. Four different kinds. I look at my face. Then I lift my shirt, unzip my jeans, and look at my belly. "Hey," I whisper. And then I cover my mouth hard, holding something in.

12

On Friday the third, I wake up at 6:57. Then I head for the bathroom. There is a chair in the way. Right. I move it, wash my hands and face, look at my watch. Ethan needs to get here. I have to go.

It's going to be positive, I know it is. I get my favorite test out of the medicine chest, bring it into the kitchen. Then back to the bathroom. Then back to the kitchen. I'll read the instructions—again—while I wait for Ethan.

After I've read the instructions twice more, I start a pot of coffee. Ethan will like that.

Seven-fifteen. What is the matter with him? What kind of a father is he?

But there, there is a knock at the door. I yank it open and Ethan says, "You didn't do it yet, did you? I'm late."

"I *know.*"

"I couldn't help it, there was an accident."

Oh, God. A bad omen.

"Nobody got hurt."

A good omen.

"Want some coffee?" I ask.

"You can't drink coffee. Didn't I tell you?"

"I didn't—it's for you."

"Oh. Thank you."

He fills a cup, and I take the pregnancy test off the kitchen table. "Okay, so . . . I'll be right back."

"Wait, do you know what to do?"

"Yes, Ethan, it's not that difficult."

"But . . . should I come with you?"

"No, I think this part I can handle unsupported."

"Okay." He sits at the kitchen table. He's a nervous wreck.

"Ethan?"

He stands up. "Yeah?"

"Take your coat off. Sit down. Relax."

"Okay." He does none of these.

I go into the bathroom, read the instructions again, sit on the toilet. All I have to do is aim, hold the stick in the "flow" for two seconds. But what if I miss? You can also catch some pee in a cup. Maybe that's safer. That's what I'll do.

I go back into the kitchen. Ethan, who has managed at least to sit down, stands back up. "Are we?"

"What?"

"Are we pregnant?"

"Ethan, I just want to say one thing, okay? I hate that 'we are pregnant' stuff. I'm the one that will be pregnant. Just me, okay? You don't have a uterus. So let's just get that clear right off the bat."

"But are we? You?"

"I didn't do the test."

"Why not?"

"Well, I'm *going* to, but I thought maybe I'd use a cup, you know, instead of aiming. Because what if I miss?"

"That's a good idea. Then you just dip it in."

"I know that, Ethan." I open the cupboard, survey the cups to see which one I should sacrifice. I need to hurry up and decide—I really do have to pee. I pull out a pink cup with a flower on it. But my mother gave me that one. I put it back, pull out my Dunkin' Donuts cup. But it's just the right size.

"Patty?"

"What?"

"Don't you have any paper cups?"

"No."

"There's good planning."

"Well, I wasn't going to *use* a cup! I just now decided to, at the spur of the moment."

"But you don't want to . . . ruin a cup, do you?"

"What else should I do? I need to catch it in something! What do you suggest?"

"Boy, are you crabby!"

"I'm not crabby! I'm nervous! Aren't you nervous? I'm nervous, and I have to *pee*!"

"Well just take a *cup,* stop *look*ing at them all!"

"But some of these are important!"

Ethan comes over to the cupboard, takes down a solid green mug. "Here. There's nothing special about this one."

"That's my Christmas cup. Every Christmas morning, I have eggnog out of it."

"I'll get you another one, okay?"

I stare at it. "Ethan?"

"What?"

"I don't think I can pee into one of my coffee cups. It's disgusting."

"Well then, pee on the stick, Patty!"

"What if I miss?"

"There are two tests in the kit, right?"

"Right." And three other tests, of course. But it seemed important that this first one be done and done right. It seemed important to just save the other tests. I have no idea why. Maybe for the baby book.

"Okay," I say. "So, I'll just go do it. I won't miss. How could I *miss*?"

"Exactly."

I go into the bathroom, and in a minute come back to the kitchen, silently go to the cupboard, and get the Christmas mug. And in a few minutes more, come back to the kitchen table and sit down with Ethan. "Want to see the stick?" I ask. He nods. I hold it up. "It's a pretty pink, isn't it?"

"It's a girl?" Ethan's voice is barely audible.

"No, no, this just means I'm pregnant."

The word fills my mouth, my neck, my chest. And, as it happens, my life.

"You are?" And then he nods, answering himself.

I start to cry a little, wipe my eyes.

"What," he says.

"Well, *you* are, too."

"What, pregnant?"

"No, crying."

"I am not," he says. But he is.

It occurs to me that this is so private, this moment. I can't wait to tell Elaine.

13

"How about 'Philip'?" Ethan says.

He is spending the night. Because it is the first day of knowing for sure and we are so excited and we have so much to talk about and we want to do it in person. Spending the night means only that; I'm not sure he'll even stay in the same bed with me. In a way, I regret our instant success. I never thought a miracle could be irritating.

Still, for the time being he is lying beside me, his shoes off, his shirt untucked, his coat hung in my closet. We ordered out for pizza and I did not get pepperoni, which is my favorite, and I did get a salad, which is not my favorite. I don't care what people say about the beauty and the taste and the virtues of vegetables, I like starch. My idea of a good meal is an egg-noodle sandwich. But I ate the damn salad. Plus I ate a carrot, at Ethan's insistence, because he found the salad "skimpy." "There's eighteen pounds of lettuce here," I told him, but he said, "No carrots. No peppers. And that cucumber looks anemic, don't eat it." He offered to eat a carrot too, to keep me company. But I declined. It felt good to be doing the right thing. Suddenly, everything I do feels like it must be passed by someone for its approval. Implantation hasn't even occurred and already I'm calling for internal conferences. And getting them. *Carrot? Why, yes, a carrot; excellent.*

"How about 'Philip'?" Ethan says again. "Huh? What do you think?"

"What did I tell you?" I say.

"Come on, we need names."

"Not *yet*."

"Oh, you're just mad because I don't like 'Eric.' "

I say nothing.

"Eric is a stupid name," he says. "Meaningless."

"Meaningless?"

"Yes."

"What exactly is the meaning of Philip?"

"The meaning of Philip is that it's a classy name."

"Oh, please. It's uptight. He'll wear those black Clark Kent glasses with no sense of irony." I sit up on the side of the bed. "Do you want to watch TV or something?"

"No. I won't suggest any more names right now, okay?"

I lie back down.

"Jesus was once an embryo," Ethan says.

I look at him, laugh.

He turns to me. "What?"

"What do you mean, 'Jesus was once an embryo'?"

"Well, He was."

I consider this, then say, "I saw Jesus the other day."

"Oh?"

"Yeah, He was in somebody's garden, a big statue of Him. He had His nice white dress on, and His rope belt; and He was holding His hands out a little bit at His sides, you know how He does, palm side up? And one leg was bent a little. He looked sort of effeminate, actually."

"Really?" Ethan asks hopefully.

"Effeminate and apologetic."

"Yeah," Ethan sighs. "We should have known better."

The phone rings, and I go to answer it. As I pick up the receiver, I think, Wow, it's true. Jesus *was* an embryo. Mozart was a ball of cells just like what is in me now. Einstein, too. Of course, Hitler, too.

"What's wrong?" my father asks, when I say hello.

"Dad! Nothing!"

"Why do you sound so glum?"

"I'm not. I was . . . doing a comp sheet. I was preoccupied. How are you?"

"Listen, honey, I want you to come over tomorrow night."

"Tomorrow?"

"Right. For dinner."

"Okay. Any particular reason?"

"I need a reason?"

"No."

"Okay, I'll give you a reason: I want you to."

"Okay. Good. So I'll bring some huge, gooey dessert for you and me?"

"Yeah, whatever you want."

"Dad?"

"Yeah."

"I was just teasing you."

"About what?"

"About dessert. You know. I know you can't have anything. No pie. Or, you know, cake. Or chocolate-chocolate chip ice cream."

He doesn't take the bait. "Whatever you want," he says again.

"Dad? Is everything all right?"

"Yeah. I'll see you tomorrow."

I go back into the bedroom. "What's up?" Ethan asks.

"I don't know," I say. "Something."

I lie down, pull a pillow over my stomach, hold it there. Then I turn to Ethan, smile. "Nothing to worry about, though, I'm sure." I don't want him to worry about anything right now. I want him to remember kissing me and think, What the hell, it's better than Scrabble.

"Hey, Patty?"

"Yeah?"

"How about 'Thomas'?"

I look away from him, sigh. "How about 'Jessica,' Ethan? You know? How about 'Margot'?"

"Oh, no. 'Lauren,' I would think, in that case."

"When should we tell people?" I ask.

"I don't know. When will we know it's . . . safe? You and the baby, I mean."

"Safe? Well, let's see. I think . . . never."

"Right. Well, let's tell anybody we want to, then."

"Want to come when I tell my parents?"

His face changes ever so slightly.

"All right," I say, "I'll do it alone. But after they know, you'll have to come over at least once so my dad can tell you how to do everything. He'll probably want to smack you on the back a lot, give you a cigar."

"You mean you think they'll be glad?"

"Yeah. I do think they'll be glad."

Ethan closes his eyes. "I'm going to wait a while to tell my mother."

I see Ethan's mother, suddenly, as clearly as though she were sitting on the bed beside us. Though of course she would not sit on the bed beside us. She would sit in a chair across the room, eyes averted. She would suggest by her body language alone that one lay in bed at *night,* to *sleep,* unless, of course, one were tending to certain obligations. She would be dressed impeccably. Her gold would be so gold. She would be just the slightest bit weary of us as soon as she saw us.

"Oh, I know you'll wait a long time to tell your mother," I say. "Maybe you can combine a birth announcement with an invitation to his college graduation."

"Oh, Jesus, Patty." He sits up.

"What?"

"We have to open a savings account."

"Yeah, we probably should."

"And apply to . . . schools!"

"What schools?"

"We don't know what we're doing."

"Well, I don't think we have to figure everything out tonight."

He gets up, crosses the room, stands at the window, looks out.

"Ethan?"

He turns to me. He looks stricken.

"Lots of people have been through this lots of times."

"Right. I know."

"And you do it . . . you know, one day at a time."

"I guess."

"Come here," I say, and, obediently, he does. When he sits beside me, I take his hand. "I'm your best friend," I say, because I don't know what else to say.

"I am all of a sudden scared to death," he says. "I'm having visions of . . . I don't know, inoculation records. Potty chairs. Orthodontists' bills."

"You're worried about money?"

"No. No. Pain. To . . . it."

"Oh," I say. "That."

Later that night, while Ethan sleeps chastely beside me, I remember sitting in my fourth-grade classroom while my teacher, the beautiful Miss Duffy, worked at her desk. I'd been excused from recess. Miss Duffy had seen how the other kids made fun of me. "Eraser face," they were calling me that week. I had no idea what that meant, but I had done some powerful imagining. I sat at my desk in the too-quiet room, drawing a neighborhood: rows of houses with window boxes, identical cars in driveways. A pie cooled on a kitchen windowsill. I didn't put any people in, their noses were too hard to draw. But evidence of their happy lives was everywhere. And their sense of belonging, that was there, too. I made *S*-shaped lines of steam rising up from the pie; I made air vents in the crust and drew the edges of cherries beneath them—I had time for such details. When I was finished, I showed Miss Duffy. She looked carefully at my drawing, and I looked carefully at her. I thought she looked exactly like Snow White. "Very nice," she said, finally, and smiled at me. Then she looked briefly out the window, longing, I knew, for the same thing I desired: for me to be out there like the rest of the girls in the class, playing hopscotch, screaming baby epithets back across the playground at the boys, replaiting Cynthia Burns's hair between turns—she had wonderful, thick black hair and did not mind people playing with it. I never was treated badly in school again; it only happened in fourth grade, for reasons I have never yet understood. Just that one year. Of course, that was enough.

14

At five-thirty, I am sitting in the obstetrician's office waiting for my four-thirty appointment, reading *Business Week*, which is not exactly my choice in reading material. But I have finished all the women's magazines, and even took a look at *Highlights*, this time concentrating less on nostalgia and more on what these stories might say to a child. For the first time, I like Gallant better than Goofus. I am walking around with a new screen on. A filter. It is a bit exhausting.

I put down the magazine, go over to the receptionist. "I'm sorry to bother you again."

"You're next," she says, not looking up.

"Is it always so long a wait?"

Now she looks up. "Dr. Carlson is a very popular doctor. One reason is that he takes his time when he needs to. You'll come to appreciate that, I'm sure. And as I told you when you arrived, he had a delivery right before office hours. That's babies for you, they operate on their own time schedule." She smiles, I suppose. To me, it looks like she's baring her teeth.

I hate when receptionists do this, when they act like they are the doctors' wives. I do understand that I am on the low end of the totem pole, not even showing. There is a definite hierarchy here, the women with the biggest bellies at last the most proud.

"Okay," I say.

"It really shouldn't be much longer," she says—kindly, this time. "If you'd like, I can put you in a room."

"No, thanks. But maybe . . . I know I'm supposed to get a blood test. Maybe I could just go ahead and do that first."

"That's a possibility." She's friendly now; we're sudden pals, working together to save time for our wonderful husband, Dr. Carlson.

The receptionist disappears, then comes back out to the waiting room. "We can do it," she says. "Right this way."

I follow her, dry-mouthed. Here we go, I'm thinking. And wish I had taken Ethan or Elaine up on their offers to come with me. I'd told them I didn't need them this time. The way Ethan is going, he probably knows more than the doctor, anyway.

The receptionist ushers me into a smallish room with a padded, recliner-type chair, a metal stool beside it. There is also a cot with shiny metal side bars and very white sheets, a pink blanket folded at the bottom. There is a cart up against the wall loaded with supplies. A hand-lettered sign below it reads RELAX! A rather stern-looking woman—brassy blonde hair in a tight ponytail, black eyeliner, drawn-in brows—comes into the room, nods at me, then asks, "You a fainter?"

"Pardon me?"

"You faint when you get blood taken?"

"I haven't yet."

"Okay, we'll put you in the big-girl chair." She raises the arm of the semirecliner, and I sit down, lean back. It feels like a ride.

"First time being pregnant?" the woman asks.

"Yes." I feel myself blushing.

"I'm Sheila," the woman says. And then, pushing my sweater sleeve up, "Make a nice fist for me, now."

I do, and she applies a tourniquet, swabs the inside of my elbow with a cold, brown liquid; snaps on gloves. Then she inserts a long needle very quickly and very nearly painlessly into my vein. "Wow," I say, watching the tubes fill up with blood. "You're good. Are you an addict or something?"

She looks up. "You can open your fist."

"Sorry," I say. "I always make bad jokes when I'm nervous."

"It's all right," she says. "It's just that . . . Yes, I was."

Oh, God.

"Just kidding," she says. Then, looking at me, "You okay?"

"Yeah," I say. "Uh-huh."

"You're a little pale. Why don't you sit here a minute?" She smiles. Badly matched crown, second molar. I really like her.

Another woman comes in, no belly on her yet, either. "You a fainter?" Sheila asks.

They see a million pregnant women. I will have to be the one to keep it all special. I crook my arm up, hold myself to myself.

"You're just in time to peel some potatoes for me," my mother says, when I walk in the door.

"Good, I'm not late, then." I take off my boots, hang up my coat. "Where's Dad?"

"Showering."

I look at my watch. "Now?"

She shrugs. "He likes to shower in the evening lately."

I put on an apron, push up my sleeves.

"It's in the top drawer," my mother says. "The . . . thing."

"What?"

"You know, the . . . slicer."

"Peeler?"

"Right."

"Okay. How many potatoes?"

"I think four, huh?" And then, seeing the Band-Aid on my arm, "What's wrong?"

"Oh!" I take the Band-Aid off. "Nothing. Just . . . blood work."

"For what? Just tell me. Oh God, you're sick, aren't you? I knew you looked different the last time I saw you. I told your father. I could see it around the eyes."

"Mom." I hadn't wanted to tell her yet, not so suddenly, certainly, but now . . . "It's . . . I had a pregnancy test."

She stands stock-still, her mouth open. And then, "You and Mark . . . ?"

"No. Me and Ethan."

" 'Ethan and I,' " she says, in a shell-shocked sort of way.

"Yes. Ethan and I. You know, I'd wanted to be a little more graceful, telling you. I wanted to tell Dad at the same time, too."

"Well," she says. And then, again, "Well. I just don't know what to say!"

I turn off the water, walk over to her, look into her face. "Are you a little happy?"

She sighs, exasperated. "Well, I . . . For one thing, is it safe? Has he been tested? And how can . . . isn't he *gay*?"

"It is safe. He's negative. And yes, he's gay."

"So did you . . . ? Well, of course, it's none of my business." She grabs the dishrag, starts cleaning off the counter.

I say nothing. This moment is huge. I feel like I need to step over it to get back to the sink. I turn the tap on again; start peeling a potato.

"Patty?"

"Yeah?" I don't turn around.

"I think we need to sit down."

I take in a deep breath as I see my father entering the room. "What's new?" he asks, kissing me. And then, seeing my face, *"What?"* He turns to my mother. "Did you tell her already?"

"Tell me what?"

"Nothing," my mother says. And looking at my father, she tells me, "We're going on a trip. We wanted to surprise you with it."

"You wanted to surprise me?"

"Yes, we thought it might be fun to have you to dinner and surprise you. Didn't we, Robert?"

"Marilyn—"

"But Patty has an even bigger surprise."

My father looks at me.

"Don't you?" she says.

"I . . . Well, yeah, I guess I do."

"Is dinner ready?" my father says. "Are we going to eat while we do this?"

Nobody around here is ready for anything. That is abundantly clear.

15

Sophia comes to my door that evening to borrow tea. She is dressed in her faded blue chenille robe and fuzzy pink slippers. Her black hair net, pulled low on her forehead, anchors the toilet tissue she has wadded up luxuriously over her ears—she calls these soft bundles her "night pillows." There is little in life more honest than one's real preference in sleepwear.

She follows me into the kitchen, and I hand her a box of Sleepytime. She inspects it, then asks, "You have some else?"

I rummage in the cupboard, hand her a box of Mandarin Orange. She smiles, shakes her head no. I pull out Wild Berry Zinger, Lively Lemon. No and no. "What are you looking for?" I ask. "Do you have something particular in mind?"

"Red Rose."

"Well, you should have said so!"

"Ah. Good. So you have."

"No, I do not. But you should have said that's what you wanted. It would have saved us both some time."

She takes in a breath, nods. "So. I am sorry to be inconvenience. A good night to you."

"Sophie," I say. "Wait. I'm sorry. I'm just in a bad mood."

She looks at the literature on pregnancy I have spread out over the kitchen table. "Some worries is start?"

"No. It's a little overwhelming, that's all. But I told my parents tonight, and they . . . didn't react the way I'd thought they might."

"How are they react?"

"I don't know. Reserved. Disappointed."

"You tell them Ethan is father, yes?"

"Well, yes. Of course."

"So. They want happy marriage, is all. And Ethan . . . "

"My mother has been telling me for a long time to just have a baby—without marriage!"

"Still, in her heart, is want for more. You will see, Patty. When there is baby, must be perfect. When is daughter, is more so."

I look at her carefully. "Do you have a daughter, Sophia?"

She looks away. "On this, I will not like to talk."

I say nothing.

She looks back at me. "I hope this is not hurting on your mind."

"Hurting my feelings?"

She nods.

"No. It's okay."

"All right. I tell you. I only *want* daughter. All in my life, this is what I want and never get. Or son, too."

"Oh, Sophia. I'm sorry."

"So. What can you do?"

I don't know what to say. The notion of someone still feeling the pain of not having children this late in life is amazing to me. And yet, when a want is so strong, why should it be surprising that it never entirely leaves? Sophia says, "You have baby come. And I can be to enjoy, too. Also help. You go out, I sit on baby. With pleasure."

"Well, I may take you up on that."

"I have honor if you do."

After Sophia leaves, I sit at the table and look through some more literature. One photograph, in a pamphlet that talks about bodily changes in pregnancy, shows what is called a *linea nigra,* a dark line running down from the belly button, which occurs in some women. I stare and stare at it, cover it with my finger, then take my finger away. I hadn't known about this. I thought the only change in pregnancy would be a gloriously rounded belly—pearlescent, perhaps. A gloriously rounded belly, and pinker cheeks, and an improved disposition. And some wisdom. Now I look at enlarged and darkened nipples, stretch marks. I lift my shirt, look around. Nothing yet.

I go to the phone, call Ethan. Again. Still not home. I had expected him to be there, to want to hear all about my doctor's visit. I liked Dr. Carlson. He was thorough, and gentle, and fine with the fact that the father was a gay man. He suggested I bring Ethan next time. He wore a beautiful, jewel-toned tie. I saw a bag of M&Ms in the pocket of his lab coat, and he shared some with me. He told me, sympathetically, that the pink vitamins he had to prescribe for me were about the size of Mary Kay Cadillacs.

I pick up the booklet called "Your Baby, Month by Month." I flip through the pages, watching the fetus develop, then turn to the very end and read a little about what to pack for the hospital. Lollipops, for a dry mouth. An outfit to bring the baby home in.

This part kills me, that you go in without a baby, and come home with one. No matter how long I'm pregnant, I don't think I'll ever believe that there is really a baby inside me until I see it. What I need is a little window right below my belly button so that I can witness the completion of an ear, the growth of real fingernails, the coming of the delicate whorl of hair at the back of the head.

Oh, I want to pack right now, fold up a tiny, soft sleeper decorated with panda bears, a yellow receiving blanket, a knit bonnet. I want to be lying in a hospital bed surrounded by flowers, holding my breathing baby, its eyes closed in sleep, its fists smelling of new flesh. I want to examine and reexamine the lineup of toes on the plump foot, the perfect arrangement of ribs and sternum protecting the working heart, the effortless bend at the very small elbow. I think pregnancy should last about three weeks, not nine months.

Although then my parents would be in Italy when the baby was born. Italy, they're going to. Or *Italia,* as my father has begun energetically calling it. They're going there because they always wanted to go and because they never had a honeymoon. I never knew that—I always thought surely they went to Niagara Falls, kissed rapturously to the thunder of the water. I was so sure about this I never even asked them about it. Now I picture them in Rome, my father saying my mother's name on some street Augustus walked on. My father is wearing a short-sleeved white shirt and shiny blue pants and one of his golf hats; his camera bumps rhythmically into his belly. My mother is wearing what she would call a decent pants suit, a sweater draped over her shoulders. She has on her prescription sunglasses and carries a map which neither of them consult.

My mother needs a vacation. She couldn't even remember my brother's phone number the other night. Of course, she was probably still upset with me. She was upset and my father was quiet. Just . . . quiet.

The phone rings, startling me. When I answer it, Ethan says, "How was the doctor?"

"Where have you been?" I say angrily. And then, hearing loud music and voices in the background, "Where are you?"

I had not meant to say that. I had not meant to feel that. He does not live here. We are not married.

"Can you come over?" I say, in a revised tone of voice. "I want to show you what they gave me at the doctor's office."

"Yeah," he says. "I was going to. I just wanted to check first. It's . . . a little late."

I look at my watch. Eleven. "I'm up."

Actually, I wasn't going to ask him to come over, either. But now I want him to see everything, to read it cover to cover, to memorize it. I want him to take a pink vitamin so large there is a breathless moment after you swallow it, when you wonder if it's going to make it down or if it's going to lie like a hammock in your esophagus. I want him to think about how he would feel if some dark line suddenly appeared on his belly, if his nipples spread out like flying saucers.

Later, lying in bed with me, Ethan says, "I can't stay here at night all the time, you know."

"I know."

"Okay, so . . . Good night."

"Good night, Ethan."

"Patty? I hope you're not offended, that I . . . that we . . ."

"No. I'm not. It's just nice to have you here. I'm not used to all of this yet, it's nice to have you to share in it."

"I do want to share in it."

"Yes."

"But . . . I still . . . you know."

"I'm not asking you to marry me, Ethan."

"I know."

"Or . . . anything."

Neither of us bothers to point to the obvious falsehood of that remark.

"Have you started getting sick yet?" Ethan asks.

"What, are you looking forward to it?"

"No."

"Not everybody gets sick."

"I know."

"Maybe I won't get sick."

"Maybe not."

"Although, I'll tell you one thing. Coffee smells pretty bad to me. Also green pepper."

"Well, that's no problem. You can't drink coffee anyway."

"No."

"Okay, so . . ." He turns onto his side.

"Ethan?"

"Yeah?"

"Did you have a date tonight?"

"I . . . Well, I met someone for a drink."

"Oh."

"It was just, you know, casual—someone wanted me to meet someone—Steven, his name was."

"Uh-huh. Did you like him?" My right hand is squeezing my left pointer to death.

"It was okay. You know. No lightning bolts."

"Do you think you'll see him again?"

"Yeah. I thought I might."

"Are you going to tell him about . . . us?"

"No, I don't think that's going to be necessary."

"No lightning bolts."

"Right." He sighs. "There hardly ever are."

"I know."

He turns toward me. "Could I feel your stomach?"

"There's nothing to feel yet."

"Well, maybe not. But I want to feel when it starts, when there is something there. I need . . . a baseline."

"Sure." I turn on my back, lift my pajama top, feel his warm palm over my stomach. I close my eyes, hold my breath, frame the moment.

"Thanks," he says, and turns back onto his side.

"You're welcome."

A few minutes later, I say, "Ethan? The only change so far is that my breasts are tender. And bigger, I think."

Silence.

"Ethan?" I whisper.

He's sleeping. Or pretending to. I move close enough to feel the heat from his body, but I am careful not to touch. You don't get everything all at once. You wait.

16

"Curly always said he'd take me to Italy," my mother says. We are standing at the window in my parents' living room, watching my father load suitcases into my car. I'm going to drive them to the airport.

"Who's Curly?"

She looks at me. "You know. James Wilkinson. We called him 'Curly' because of his beautiful blond hair. He was one of my boyfriends in high school."

"You never told me."

"Well, I'm sure I did, Patty!"

"Well, I for*got,*" I say, but I didn't. She never told me.

"I always thought I'd see Curly again . . . some high school reunion, something. I used to think about how I'd run into him and he'd still be so handsome. And maybe he would still . . . you know, carry a torch, just a little." She comes away from the window, sits on the sofa. "I figured it would be just once, sometime. We'd be old, but . . . " She sighs.

"Is he dead?"

She looks up. "Curly? Oh no. My friend Betty Hall, you remember *her*?"

I nod, relieved that I do.

"She lives near him in Arizona. Sees him all the time, runs into him different places. He still asks for me every now and then, can you imagine?"

"So . . . you *could* see him again."

She picks at the hem of her skirt. "I don't think so."

"Dad wouldn't care."

"No."

"So . . . ?"

She looks at her watch. "We should go. Not much time."

"We have plenty of time."

She smiles at me, sadly, as though I've told a joke that isn't so funny after all.

"How are you feeling?" she asks, suddenly.

"Fine. Just a little tired."

"When we come back, you'll be almost four months. You'll have a little belly!"

"I know."

"So maybe we'll . . . I don't know, have a little party."

"Okay."

"You want to miss the plane, Marilyn?" my father yells in the door. "Is that what you want? Because if you don't get out here, we're going to miss the plane! What are you *do*ing?"

My mother looks at me. "I wouldn't mind missing the plane," she says.

She is a mystery so often, now.

• • •

At the airport, I drop my parents off, then go to park the car. My father told me there was no need to come in, but I want to. I am aware of the fact that there are some times in life that point toward the possibility of danger more than others, and as far as I'm concerned, flying is one of them. How could I just drop my parents off and then be telephoned later and told of their fiery crash? Of course, the downside of my well-intentioned hanging around is that it's boring as hell for everyone. Looking at clocks becomes everyone's temporary obsession—though for me, of course, there's nothing temporary about it. In fact perhaps the real reason I like to wait for people's flights to be called is that it's a comfort to be in a big place with people who look at their watches almost as often as I do.

I find my parents by the Dunkin' Donuts cart. "Want a coffee, Patty?" my father asks, handing one to my mother, then collecting his own.

"I can't have any."

"Why not?"

I look at him, exasperated.

"What?" he asks. Then, stepping closer to me and lowering his voice, "You don't like Dunkin' Donuts? You want another kind?"

"I can't drink it because of the baby."

He looks around. "What baby?"

I look at my mother for help, but she acts as puzzled as my father.

"You can't have coffee when you're pregnant," I tell them.

"Who says?" my mother asks.

My father's posture becomes erect. "Your mother had coffee with all four of you kids. I don't see any problems with any of you. You see any problems, Marilyn?"

My mother waves her hand. "Oh, who can keep up? Coffee's bad for you; coffee's all right. Beef is poison; beef is okay."

"Beef is okay?" my father asks.

"Never mind," my mother says.

"Sir?" the woman at the coffee cart says. "Is that all, two coffees?"

"Oh, sorry." He hands her a five-dollar bill. Then he asks, "Is this coffee . . . organic?"

The woman hands him back his change. "Pardon me?"

"Is this coffee organic. You know. Is it safe?"

She stares at him. "Yes sir, it's safe."

"So it's organic."

"Well, that . . . I have no idea." She looks with relief at the sight of another customer approaching.

We walk over to a seating area, sit down, me opposite them. I look at my watch, feel my leg start to jiggle, stop it.

"I swear," my mother says, "you listen to all they say about everything and you'll lose your mind. You just have to use some common sense. Half the time they don't really know what they're talking about, they're just guessing."

"Well," I say, "you also have to try to be careful when you're pregnant. You want to give the baby the best possible start, right? And if you hear that something's possibly dangerous, and you don't need it, then why take a chance?"

My mother stares past me. I see the wide angle of the plateglass window reflected in her blue eyes. An airplane bisects the angle, heading practically straight up. I turn around to watch it with her.

"We're going to wake up in Rome," she says, with a kind of sad wonder.

"Roma!" my father says. "We'll eat pasta for breakfast."

"All I want to do is relax," my mother says, and, as though in ironic counterpoint, her hands tighten on her purse.

"I need to pee," I say. "I'll be right back."

My mother stands. "I'll come, too."

"I'll be right here," my father says, unnecessarily.

"What's that, Robert?"

"I'll be here," he says again. "By the doughnut cart."

"Right."

I smile conspiratorially at my mother as we walk away. But she doesn't smile back.

After I get home, I lie down. I'm sleepy, and feeling a little ragged around the edges. There's something about airports that always makes me feel bad. The weeping at the leave-takings. The joy at the reunions. These are painful things for someone like me, who returns home nightly to no one, who bids good-bye every morning to a blank kitchen wall.

In the airport bathroom, as my mother and I stood washing our hands, our eyes met in the mirror. "I'll miss you," she said, in a way that was almost shy.

"Me too," I said.

"Water that ficus carefully. It *acts* like it wants a lot, but it doesn't."

"Right." I had no idea what she was talking about. For as long as I can remember, my mother has had relationships with plants far too complicated for me to understand. She uses eggshell water to nourish certain plants; Chopin études to stop the yellowing of leaves on others.

"And the African violets, you know how they are, you just keep that gravel at the bottom of their pots damp."

"I will."

When we were walking out, my mother saw a sign for a Nursing Room. "Look at that," she said.

I nodded.

"I've never seen that before! Have you?"

Again, I nodded.

"You want to go in?"

I smiled.

She pushed open the door. I expected to see a mother whose countenance resembled the Madonna, and who, upon learning I was pregnant, would offer invaluable advice. But the room was empty. My mother sat on the little leatherette sofa, patted the space beside her.

"I didn't nurse you," she said, after I sat down.

"I know."

"I'm sorry."

"It's all right. In those days, they probably told you the bottle was better."

"No, it was . . . " She looked away. "Well, I had inverted nipples."

I so much did not want to hear anything about that. My mother's body needs to be permanently clothed in my mind.

Preferably in a housedress and an apron. I was blushing as furiously as she. "Oh, well," I said, finally, "what are you going to do?"

"But I think you should nurse your baby. I know it's not really my place to tell you, but from everything I've read—"

"I'm going to."

"All right."

My mother leaned back, crossed her arms, stared busily straight ahead.

"Mom?"

"Yes."

"Don't you think we should go?"

She stared blankly at me for a moment, then said, "Well, I thought a little rest from your father would be nice, that's all. He's going to start quoting from the phrasebook any minute, I just know it."

"He's excited."

She sighed. "Yes."

"Don't you want to go, Mom?"

She stood, pulled her purse up over her shoulder. "Well, of course I do. It's just that . . . I've worked very hard trying to make a life I love."

"I know you have."

"So why would I want to leave it?"

"Well, you're not *leav*ing it."

"Of course I am."

"Mom, you're going on va*ca*tion. To Italy. Which is beautiful."

"I know that, Patty. It's just that I can't imagine liking anyplace better than where I live."

"Oh, stop," I said, standing. "You're turning into such a curmudgeon!" I held open the door for her. "You said yourself you really want to relax."

"Well, that's true. That's absolutely true. God knows I need that." She went out the door at the same time that a mother carrying a baby and a huge diaper bag came in. They smiled at each other.

"Dang," I said quietly, once we were both outside the room. "I wanted to watch."

"Do you really think she wouldn't mind?" my mother asked.

"I don't know," I said. "Everything's different now. It used to be that having a baby was so routine. Now so often it's . . . a triumph."

I should know, I don't need to add. I still haven't let myself take in my own gratefulness, my wonder at my pregnant self. I'm too afraid to admit it wholly, I suppose. Because there is always the possibility I could not have a baby after all—I could miscarry; I could deliver a stillborn. I read about these horrors nightly, though Ethan has warned me against it. But I can't help it. Once I called him at work and said, "What if I have an incompetent cervix?" First he said, "Who's calling?" Ha, ha. Then he said, "If you have an incompetent cervix, they'll suture it closed." He thinks he knows everything. He probably does. He keeps a virtual library on pregnancy and childbirth on his bedside table. "Do you hide this when you have . . . guests?" I once asked. "I suppose I would," he said, thus answering both my questions.

As my mother and I walked slowly down the airport hall, I said, "I think a lot of people are so happy to have babies now they relish the opportunity to share everything. I'll tell you one thing. I really wanted to see what was in that diaper bag."

"Well, diapers of course," my mother began, then stopped, exasperated, and waved back at my father. He had left his chair to gesture hugely at us, as though he were directing in one of the jumbo jets outside.

"We *see* you, Robert!" she said.

"You see me?"

"Yes!"

"Well, fine." He sat back down, looked into his cup of coffee, then threw it away.

When I hugged him good-bye, he said quietly into my ear, "She'll be much better when she gets back."

"Oh, I know," I said, as though I suddenly understood everything.

Now I get up, stand at the window, and look across the street. The children who live there have decorated all the windows with red construction-paper hearts in honor of Valentine's Day. When my parents came over last week, my mother said, "Well, look at that. That house has the measles."

There was some humor in it. Some poetry. And something else that was not funny or poetic, but chilling. Her seriousness in saying it. Something that suggested she might really believe it.

17

Ethan and I are the only guests sitting at our table at Elaine's reception. We may, in fact, be the only guests sitting at all—the band is great. But I am a terrible dancer, and Ethan is keeping me company. The tablecloth is a heavy ivory linen; the flowers in the centerpiece exquisite. I want them when I leave, and I keep watching them, in case someone else has the same idea.

The service was beautiful: simple and sincere. Elaine looked lovely, needless to say; Mark looked very, very handsome; and my heart lurched a bit at the sight of him putting the ring on her finger. I expected it might—I swallowed and smiled and felt as if a line of pain was being pulled continuously out of my middle. I am amazed at how quickly this all happened—only a few months ago, she was telling me she might get married.

The reception is populated by smiling and beautifully dressed guests, all of whom seem ecstatic at this sudden union. "Do you think maybe she's pregnant?" one matronly and fairly well-lubricated guest asked me. "No, *she's* not," I said, and was greatly disappointed that there was no follow-up question that would let me reveal happy news of my own. I watched the matron walk away, thinking of how we could have had an exciting chat about me. "It's *Elaine's wed*ding," Ethan said quietly into my ear at that point, as though he were reading my mind. "I am aware of that," I said back, and then added, "Why don't you go find some little friends to play with?"

"Do you see any little friends for me?" he asked. I had to admit I did not.

Now I look at the fashionable styles going by, and at the small, tidy waists. My bridesmaid dress is cut quite a bit differently from the others, allowing for the bulge that is unmistakably there, but not quite unmistakably pregnancy. I look like someone who has been romancing potato chips a little too often—and, if the truth be told, I have been. If I have to endure four to five servings of vegetables a day, I get a compensatory bag of chips every now and then. Dr. Carlson said I could, though Ethan took exception to that advice. Everything else about Dr. Carlson Ethan loves. After he met him, he said on the way home, "Did you see his shoes? Ferragamos." And then, casually, "He doesn't wear a wedding ring, did you notice?" "He has two children," I answered. And then, before Ethan could say, "*Well* . . ." I added, "And a beautiful female wife."

A man dancing with a woman close to our table dips her dramatically; then they laugh. So many people are laughing—I hear a veritable symphony of staccato bursts of hilarity, pretty feminine trills, hearty belly laughs.

"I find this so depressing," Ethan says.

"Exactly."

"It makes me feel so . . . unskilled."

"Yes."

Elaine's mother stops by our table. "Having a good time?" she asks us.

"Oh yes!" I say, and Ethan nods so enthusiastically I'm afraid she's going to think he has a bit of a disability.

After she leaves, he says, "I'm going home."

"Oh, Ethan, it's not that bad!"

"It's wonderful for people who have someone. For those of us who are still looking—unsuccessfully—and are so *tired* of it . . . You know, I've been to three weddings in the last month."

"Really?"

"Yeah, remember I told you about Ed and Paul? And then there was another one the week after. Michael and Alex, you never met them. I dated Alex for a while."

I watched Elaine and Mark step toward each other for a slow dance. They are smiling, each filling up the other. "You were crazy about Alex," I tell Ethan. "I remember you talking about him. He had gray eyes that were so beautiful."

Ethan sighs. "Yeah."

"And an amazing body. And that voice."

"Do you mind?"

"Sorry."

He stands up. "You want to leave with me?"

"No, I'll stay for a while."

He looks at his watch. "It's late. Eleven-forty."

"Just for a little more. I'm not quite ready to leave."

"I don't know why."

"Don't be so nasty. Go get some sleep or something."

After he leaves, I take a glass of champagne from a roving waiter. One sip won't hurt anybody. Of course, it won't help anybody either.

After I am in bed, the phone rings. I look at the clocks. Two-fifty. When I answer, I hear Ethan say, "Well, weren't we out late?"

"Yeah." I smile, yawn. I'm so relieved no one's dead.

"Where have you been?"

"Excuse me?"

"Where have you been?"

"First of all, I don't like your tone of voice. Secondly, I don't think it's any of your business."

"Oh, I would say it is my business. Yes, I would say it definitely is."

"Why?"

"Because you are carrying my baby."

I feel a confusing mix of anger and joy.

"And?" I manage to say.

"And I want you to be . . . safe. So that the baby's safe. Were you drinking?"

"Yes. I had a sip of champagne."

"Oh, great."

"Ethan, I'm being literal. I had one sip."

"That's exactly how it starts."

"How *what* starts?"

"Not taking care of yourself. You know? Not being careful.

First it's a sip, then it's a glass, then the baby comes out with wings."

"Ethan."

"What?"

"Don't you think you're getting a little carried away?"

"Well, what were you *do*ing so late? I've been trying to call you for hours. It's not good for you to run yourself down."

"I can sleep all day if I want to, Ethan! I was having a conversation with some guy I met, okay? He was just a really nice guy, fun to be with, and the time got away from us. Everybody stayed at the reception until one-thirty, and then Jeff and I went to get something to eat."

"Jeff, is it?"

"Yes, Jeff it is."

"Does he know you're pregnant?"

"No."

Jeff was definitely not my type—about fifty pounds overweight and a good six inches shorter than I and wildly in love with his fiancée, who was out of town, but this is something I see now I might do well to keep to myself.

"Don't you think you should tell him you're pregnant?"

"I will . . . eventually."

"You can't sleep with him, you know, it's too dangerous."

"You can have sex all the way through pregnancy!"

"No, you can't."

"Ethan, what is your *problem*? You date!"

"Hardly ever."

"But you *do*."

He is quiet for a long moment, and then he says, "I think we should move to Minneapolis."

"What?"

"I think we should move there."

"*Why?*"

"I think we should try to live together. And I can't do it here. I think we should do it there."

"But—"

"I got offered a transfer there. And a raise. You can take some time off from working, don't you want to do that? It's pretty there. It's safe. And I want to be somewhere where we can try . . . where I'm not . . ."

"Ethan, what are you saying?"

"I don't know. I'm happier when I'm with you. I care about the baby, I think about it all the time."

"I know you care about the baby."

"I want to . . . I want it to think I'm its father."

"You *are* its father!"

"I know. But I want it to feel me. I need to be around it more."

"So move in here."

"No, it has to be . . . Patty, will you just try this? You can keep your apartment, let's just go there and try it, at least for a few months, will you? I told them I'd be willing to transfer as long as I could come back if I wanted to. There's no risk. You can take time off. No offense, but I hardly think they'd know the difference."

"I sell things!" I say. I hope he doesn't ask me when the last one was.

"Yes, but I think you could take some time off, don't you?"

I look out the window. Ethan is asking me to live with him somewhere where nobody knows us. He is asking me to live with him. Suppose I were lying around some idle afternoon reviewing my Wish List. Would this not be on it? Is there any real reason to refuse? "Okay," I say.

"I'll come over tomorrow," he says. "We'll figure everything out."

"You could come now. Tonight."

"Tomorrow, okay? For breakfast."

I hang up the phone, start to call Elaine, and remember she's on her honeymoon. For a moment, I consider calling her anyway. But I don't. I lie awake, seeing if the ceiling has any idea how all this has come about.

18

After my mother and I finish the dinner dishes, I head for the living room to tell my father and Ethan that dessert is ready. I stop just before going into the room; my father is speaking in a low and confidential tone that means I should leave and come back later. But I edge in closer, then lean back against the wall so that I can see without being seen. My chest is full of the excitement I used to feel playing hide-and-seek when I saw the seeker's shoes right beside me and pushed my face into my hands, squeezed my eyes shut, and held my breath. I hope my mother doesn't catch me. She'll ask me if this is the way she raised me and I'll have to say no, it is not.

"I'm going to tell you something, young man," my father says, settling back in his chair. "There comes a time in your life when you just don't give a shit anymore. You know what I mean?"

Ethan sits leaning forward, his fingers linked loosely between his knees. The light from the lamp picks up highlights in his hair, outlines his profile. If I know him for eighty more years, if I see him every day for the rest of my life, he will still take my breath away at random moments. I put my hand to my belly, think, *have* his *hair, okay?*

"You know what I mean?" my father repeats.

"I think so."

"Huh?" my father asks loudly.

"Yes," Ethan says. "I know what you mean."

"All right. There comes a time when you're not trying to prove *any*thing. You read me?"

"Yes, sir."

I smile at this, Ethan calling my father "sir" just because he knows how much Dad likes it.

"Now, I don't believe that's happened to you yet," my father says—kindly, really.

"I don't think so."

"Right, because you know when it *will* happen? When it will really happen?"

"When?"

"When you become a father."

Silence.

"When you hear your baby cry for the first time, you're going to understand something like you never understood it before. I guarantee you."

"Yes, sir, maybe so."

"I'm telling you, I know so. Because when you hear that baby cry, your heart will practically break wide open with your all of a sudden just . . . *know*ing. All right? You're going to understand that something is here now that you can never again be without. Something that matters more than anything. And I'm telling you . . . When Patty was born, I cried more than she did. And I'm not ashamed to admit it, either. That's what will happen to you, too. You know what I mean?"

My eyes tear; I put a finger to each corner. Lately, if I'm not laughing uproariously at things that are only slightly funny, I'm weeping.

"Yes, sir, I think I know what you mean."

"Everybody will be bawling, huh?!"

"Right."

"And that," my father says, speaking quietly again, "is when you grow up, son. I'm telling you. Right then. The reason for everything is all of a sudden right in front of you. You're holding it."

I can't stand it any longer. I come into the room. "Dad? You want dessert?"

Dad? Do you know how much I love you?

He turns to me and I see him looking at me on the day I was presented to him. I know how his arms held me. I can feel it again. I swear I can feel it exactly, the straight line of his arm beneath my new back, the cupping of his hand under my head. I can see him, too—his rolled-up sleeves, his messy hair, his eyes directed at something he will never stop seeing.

"Sure, honey," he tells me now. "We'll have some dessert." And then, to Ethan, "You ready?"

Ethan smiles, nods. I believe he is incapable of speaking. And that is yet another reason I love Ethan Allen Gaines. *Have his heart,* I think.

My mother is sitting at the kitchen table, chin in her hands, when we come into the room. She starts, then stands, ready to serve.

"Sit down," I say. "I'll do it."

"That was a very good dinner," Ethan says, sitting opposite my parents.

"Thank you." My mother smiles at him, nods.

"Really delicious," he says. And then, "Patty and I are going to move to Minneapolis."

My parents turn to look at me. I can feel their eyes on me, but I can't quite look up from serving the angel food cake.

"You can't be serious," my father says.

"Well," I say. And then, into the heavy silence, "We were thinking we'd like to try living somewhere different." I sit down.

" 'We,' " my mother says. *"We?"*

"Well, yes, we'd be living together," I say. "There. You know, in Minneapolis."

"You can die in those winters!" my father yells.

"Well, of course, it is spring," I say and wish Ethan would help me out here now that he has created a disaster. *Talk,* I think.

And he does. "I thought I might try to act a little . . . straight."

Now my parents turn to look at him, again in unison, as though they are being choreographed by a highly unimaginative director. He smiles at them, shrugs. I can't say anything. I am very busy remembering a game I used to play when I was around four. I would climb up on a chair with a beach ball and drop it on my family of stand-up paper dolls. Who knows what motivated me to do it? I loved those paper dolls. But I chose the beach ball because I knew that with it, I couldn't miss.

"This is an absolutely ridiculous idea," my father says, standing. "You don't need to go running off to some godforsaken place. Why don't you try to change right here? Be a man about it!" He hikes his pants up emphatically.

"Well, there's a certain . . . history here," Ethan says. "It would be hard to live a different kind of life."

"A certain *his*tory, huh?" My father sits back down, leans in toward Ethan. "Now, you listen to me, son. I don't hold it against you, your . . . I say a man is entitled to live his life as he sees fit when he's living for himself. But now you're talking about dragging my pregnant daughter into all this with you."

"Dad," I say.

"Never mind! There's no reason for you to move! It's not a good idea to move now!"

"Robert!" my mother says quickly.

A moment, and then, ". . . What?" I say. "Why isn't it a good idea?"

"Oh, he just doesn't want you to go. You're the last child left here. He's just being selfish. You're being selfish, Robert."

"*Mar*ilyn—"

"No," she says. And then, to me, "Do you want to go, honey?"

I don't answer.

"Do you think it might be . . . better?" she asks quietly. And with that it is the two of us alone and she is sitting at the side of my bed in her skirt and ironed blouse and cardigan sweater, her legs crossed, her hands folded in her lap. I am lying down in my realest nightgown and wildest hairdo, my arm across my eyes, shredded Kleenex in a wet pile beside me. We have finished a long and extremely difficult conversation during which I have revealed everything—everything—as though I were removing detritus from my soul, then dusting it off and lining it up on the windowsill for her inspection, just as I used to do with wildflowers, with seashells and valentines, with glass jewelry from the gumball machines outside Woolworth's. And, as always, she has seen it. And she has tenderly handled each thing to show me that she sees it, and that she knows.

I do what people almost always do in situations where gratefulness is more than we can bear: almost nothing. I nod. Sniff.

"Well, then," she says. She stands up, goes to put her cup in the sink. "Minnesota is not so far away." She looks at my father, smiles. "It's *not*."

My father sighs, looks at me. "Are you really going to do this, honey? You don't even know how to fish. All they've got there is lakes."

"I thought we'd try it," I say. "I can always come back."

"You know, I think maybe I said this all wrong," Ethan says, as though he can start over.

I am lying in bed, just ready to slip over the blurry line into sleep. Ethan drifted off over an hour ago; I listened jealously to his even breathing, hoping that he would start snoring so I could poke him and wake him up.

We looked at places for rent in Minneapolis before we went to bed tonight, sat at the kitchen table squinting at the poor-quality faxes I'd brought home from the office of high-rises, duplexes, and tiny single-family houses. We talked about that so we wouldn't have to talk about anything else, namely what he means by "acting straight."

"Look!" I said, about one place. "I think this is where Mary Tyler Moore lived, after she moved!"

"No big apartment buildings; I don't want so many neighbors," Ethan said.

"But Mary Tyler Moore lived there! She and Mister Grant tried kissing there!"

"She didn't really live there, Patty."

"I know, but—"

"Don't you like this place on Lake Minnetonka?"

I looked at it. "I don't think I can live in a place near a lake with a name like that."

"Well, I'm afraid the lakes all have names like that."

"No. There's a Lake Harriet."

"Too old-maid-auntish."

"And a Lake Calhoun."

" 'Calhoun' doesn't even *go* with a lake!"

"Well, you're the one who wants to live there!"

"Yes, but for the Democrats!"

"I think you nearly killed my parents tonight, Ethan."

"Speaking of Democrats?"

I didn't answer.

"I know. I was wondering when we'd get to that. I'm sorry."

"Well."

"I'll fly them out to visit us as soon as we're moved in. And when the baby's born, of course."

"I'm going to bed," I said. "Are you coming?" The words had a richness in my mouth like chocolate. He looked up, and I saw the answer there. Yes, he was coming to bed. No, not for that. Not yet, I thought, that's all he means. One thing at a time, that's all.

Now I feel something like a flash of nausea zip through my stomach. Morning sickness, I think? Now?

Again. A sensation of . . . no, *not* nausea. Of . . . a goldfish swimming. Of something wrong? Of something wrong?

"Ethan?" I say.

"Hmmm?"

"Wake up!"

He turns over. "What is it? What happened?"

I sit up, turn on the light, remember. "Oh," I say.

"What?"

"It's . . . I'm feeling the baby move. It moved in me, and I felt it. Quickening, that's what it is."

He sits up, his face pale.

"No, it's good. It's good."

"I *know.* Do you think I can I feel it?"

"I don't think so."

"Can I try?"

"Of course."

He puts his hand gently to my belly, then stills as though feeling by listening. After a while, he shrugs, lies back down.

"You'll feel it pretty soon," I say. "It will start kicking." It will start kicking!

"Does it hear yet?"

"I don't know. I think so."

He presses his face to my stomach, speaks quietly. "Hey, it's me. Your father, Ethan." He looks up at me. "I hope he speaks English.

"Do you speak English?" he asks my belly. Then, so softly I can barely hear him, "I love you."

He rolls onto his back, closes his eyes, and I close mine.

"Patty?"

"Yeah?"

"How about 'David'?"

"Oh, God, Ethan, go to sleep."

"Is he still moving?"

"He went back to sleep. He heard you starting up with the names again."

"Listen, would you mind if we got a cat in Minneapolis?"

"Not a Himalayan," I say quickly.

"Why not?" he asks, wounded.

"Well . . . too many memories, I would think."

"Yeah, I guess."

"We'll go to the animal shelter. We'll get a Minneapolis orphan kitty."

"How about 'Kitty'? It's good. Retro. Don't you think?"

"Good night, Ethan."

19

"Call me when the baby's born; I'll fly out there and give it its first manicure," Amber says. "We'll use 'Newborn Pink'; it's a real color." She leans back to admire her work thus far. "Awesome. There's nothing like pregnancy to fire up your fingernails."

"And hair," I say, patting my newly done coiffure.

"Right, hair, too. You look good, Patty."

"Thank you."

"So. You all packed?"

"Yeah. It feels so strange."

"I'll bet."

Something about her tone seems ominous. "What?" I say.

She looks up. "Huh?"

"What do you mean? You sound like . . . I don't know, what *do* you mean?"

"Well. You have to admit . . . "

"What?"

She screws on the top of the nail polish, turns the light of her nail dryer on. I put my hands in, lean back, look at her.

She sighs. "I just mean . . . how much faith do you have that this can really work?"

"Well . . . It was his idea. I guess I have a lot of faith that it can work."

"Okay."

"He's not saying he's going to immediately become heterosexual or anything. We're just going to live together as . . . Well, I don't know what as. He just wants to live . . . without some things for a while."

"Yeah." She leans in. "That's the part I have a little trouble with."

"What do you mean?"

"What does *he* mean? I think . . . Well. You tell me if I'm out of line, here, Patty, okay?"

"Okay." You're out of line, I'm thinking.

"I think this is a smoke screen for something else going on with Ethan. He's running away into you, you know what I mean? Into you and the baby. He's running away from something."

"I don't think he's running away from something. He just wants a quieter life. He wants the baby to know him. He wants to live together so he'll be more involved, more present. And he can't do it here. He wants someplace new, a clean start." I take my nails out of the warmer.

"You're not done," Amber says.

"I'm done," I say. And then, "I'm sorry. I'm not mad at you. But I think . . . maybe we shouldn't talk about it. I'm happy about it. I don't want to ruin it."

"Patty?"

"Yeah."

"I want to tell you something. A couple of things. One, I'm your friend."

"I know, Amber."

"No. I mean it, I really feel like I'm your friend. And if, when you have the baby, you can use some help, you call me. I'll come. I mean it. I'm good at that stuff—making meals, cleaning, staying out of the way when the people need time. . . . Really."

"Well . . . God, Amber. Thank you." My eyes fill and I dab at them. "Sorry. I'm a crying fool."

"It's the hormones," she says.

"I know."

"Watch the polish."

"I am."

"The other thing I want to tell you, Patty, is this." She hesitates, then says, "Are you listening?"

"Yes." I nod, finish wiping tears away.

"Be careful with your heart, kid. You know what I'm saying?"

"Yes. I know what you're saying. But I don't know how you ever do that, really. Do you?"

She smiles. "I guess not."

I stand, pick up my purse, my new jacket. It's a sage green maternity jacket Ethan got at some designer store, and he probably paid at least four hundred dollars for it. He says if he doesn't shop for me I'll end up wearing stuff like T-shirts with arrows pointing to the stomach that say, "Baby." "What's so bad about those T-shirts?" I asked when he told me, and he said, "Do me a favor. Let me buy your clothes. And . . . if you don't mind, I'll put together the baby's wardrobe, too."

"Fine," I said, miffed, until I realized what a good deal it was.

"I'll really miss you, Amber," I say now.

"Hey," she says, shrugging.

"I'll call you."

"The second it's born, okay?"

"Before that. I'll need a color consult, I'm sure."

"Tip from the trade: whatever you see in the magazines is passé."

I hug her, put a twenty-dollar bill down on her table.

She picks it up, hands it back to me. "Get out of here. What do you want to insult me for? This was on the house, your good-bye present, a farewell manicure. Don't fucking *chip* it, either."

"I'll be careful," I tell her.

"Oh, this is creepy," Elaine says, eyeing the stacks of packed boxes.

"I know. That's what Sophia said. Only the word she used was 'feely.' "

"Well . . . that too, I guess."

Sophia helped me pack almost everything. When we got to the dishes, she said, "I like this. Now I am feel like china shopwoman in fancy place." When we finished packing, she hugged me so hard I felt breathless. "I wish I never see you again," she said quietly into my ear. I stepped back, laughing. "What do you mean?"

"I hope you find there some happiness that you do not come back."

"But I'll come back to visit," I said. "And you wanted to baby-sit."

"Yes. Okay. That was when was a different story. Now, to live here, you by yourself, this is over."

"Well, not yet. I'm keeping the place for a few months. This is an experiment, really."

"An experiment."

"Yes, you know, to just try something."

"I don't think is so experiment for you," she said.

Now Elaine asks, "Is the furniture all you're leaving?"

"Well, no. Most of my clothes are still here. Borrow them if you want."

"Yeah. No thanks."

"You and Ethan. Textile snobs." I sit down on a box, look around.

"Are you leaving your books?" Elaine asks.

"All of them except for the ones about pregnancy."

"I might borrow some books."

"Okay."

This comforts me, somehow, the notion of Elaine over here, her head bowed over my bookshelf. Keeping my place, so to speak.

"I'll have to visit right away," she says. "Call me when you're all unpacked so I don't have to do any work."

"I will."

She bites at her lip, then says, "Let's go eat; I hate looking at this."

I turn out the lights, let Elaine go out first. Then, before I close the door, I turn back and look at the boxes and remember something I heard recently on a voice-activated telephone. "*Rea*dy," it kept saying. "*Rea*dy."

20

Thirty miles outside of the Twin Cities, it hits me that I'm really moving. I have never lived anywhere but Crystal Cove, with the exception of the time I spent in Boston going to school. And even then I came home for at least half of the weekends. I was ashamed of this; I used to lie and say I was going other places, but I wanted to be home. I liked where I came from. I still do. I'm resigned to myself by now: if I find a cheese I like, I never feel compelled to try another. Same with restaurants. When I saw Kris Kristofferson in *A Star Is Born,* I related to him because the only movie he ever went to was *Gone With the Wind*—because he knew it was good.

Now, everywhere I look is something I don't recognize. I feel a mild sense of panic, relieved by the sight of Ethan's hands on the steering wheel. I suppose Ethan is another kind of cheese, if you know what I mean.

"What are we going to do when we get there?" I ask him.

"Look at a few places to live, I guess, don't you think?" He looks over at me. "Is that what you meant?" He has circles under his eyes; he's been waking up a lot at night. As have I. Last night I lay awake a good forty-five minutes watching headlights sweep across the motel wall. Every time I closed my eyes, I felt as though I were still moving. There was an occasional drip from the bathroom faucet that I silenced around three-thirty by putting a towel in the sink. The rug smelled like Fritos; something we found amusing at first, then irritating. "I hate that smell, it's too close to feet," Ethan said, and I said maybe it *was* feet and he said great, thanks for saying so, that helped a lot.

"You know," I tell him now, "Amber said something interesting about you."

"I never met her."

"I know, but we've talked about you. And she has an interesting take on why you're doing this, why you're moving here with me."

"Is that right." His voice is cool, neutral.

"Yeah, she thinks you're just running away from something. That you're less interested in getting involved with the baby than getting uninvolved with something else."

"Do you remember where we're supposed to exit?"

I pick up the map. "I don't think we ever said."

"Well, we need to de*cide,* Patty." There is a sudden and unpleasant edge to his voice.

"What's wrong with *you*?"

He looks at me. "I'm lost, okay? I'm driving. I need to pay attention to where we're going, here. Let's analyze my motives later. For now, let's just get to where we're going. Is that all right with you? With you and Amber?"

I hate when you've made a commitment to do something with

someone, when you've maybe even burned some bridges to do it, and then they start getting weird on you. I especially hate it when you're pregnant and that happens. I start to get a little sad. A lot sad, actually.

Thank God I kept my apartment.

"I need a bathroom," I say, though I don't. I just want to stop. I just want to get out of the car and walk away from him and our stupid U-Haul and go into a bathroom and look at my face and say, "What in the world were you thinking?"

Ethan pulls into a Mobil station/restaurant, parks next to the bathrooms. When I open the door, he says, "Wait." And then, "I'm sorry. I'm . . . scared."

"Is that it?"

"Well, you are too."

"I'm not scared, I'm disappointed."

"At what?"

"At . . . *this.* I thought it would be fun! It's exciting, going to a new place. This could be a very good thing for both of us. It was your idea! And now you're just sitting there getting more and more uptight, Ethan, I can feel it. We started out really talking, making plans. . . . Now that we're getting close, you're getting quieter and quieter. Listen, I'll go back. I don't care. Just turn the car around. Take me back. You don't need to be involved in this at all. I'll do it myself. I think I'd like that better, anyway."

Someone knocks on my window, startling me: a huge man, a trucker, dressed in a grease-stained shirt, saggy blue jeans, and a black leather jacket festooned with chains. "You want to get this car the fuck out of the way so that I can get my rig past?" he says.

"You want to watch your language?" Ethan asks.

"*Eth*an," I say. I don't think he can quite see this guy. But he will in a minute because the guy's going over to his side of the car.

The trucker leans down, looks in at Ethan. He has a balding head, a reddish-colored beard going a few different directions, the small, mean eyes of a pig. "You got a fucking problem with my fucking language, fuckhead?"

Ethan turns the engine off. "Go ahead, Patty," he says. "I'll be waiting here with Mr.—" he squints at the man's name, embroidered on his shirt—"Ah. Sandy. Nice name. Effeminate, but nice."

"I don't have to go anymore," I tell Ethan quickly. I slam the car door, put my seat belt back on.

"Well, did you want a snack?" Ethan asks me. "I might want some . . . oh, I don't know, what do you recommend, Sandy? Beef jerky?"

"Here's what I recommend. I recommend you get this car out of the way before I mess up your face a little. Why don't you do that?"

"Why *don't* I?" Ethan says. "Well, let's see. Because you offended my wife?"

Sandy straightens, starts pounding his fists down on top of the car. The warm-up act, I presume.

I cover my ears, find myself midpoint between laughing and screaming. "Let's *go*!"

And thank God, Ethan starts the car, drives away.

"What was *that*?" I say, when we are safely back on the freeway. "What were you *do*ing?"

"I don't know. Did you like it?"

I start to laugh. "Yes. John *Wayne*!"

"Yeah." He turns on the radio. The unfamiliar voice of the DJ starts talking about the Vikings. Ethan and I look at each other and he takes my hand. I stop breathing, stare out the window, start taking in this new place as though it were homework. *My wife!* the back of my brain is thinking. I might send Amber a postcard with a brief message: You were wrong. No offense.

The duplex, located in a small suburb west of Minneapolis, is furnished with a sofa, two chairs, a dinette set, and a bed. Enough to get started. Right across the street is Lake Minnetonka, which looks to me nearly as vast as the ocean I've left behind. There is a small balcony, accessible through sliding-glass doors that go across the length of the living room, and Ethan and I stand on it now to discuss things. Inside, the realtor uses his cellular phone to persuade some home owner that the best offers come right away, they shouldn't hold out much longer than a few weeks for a better offer. Not always true, of course, but as I am temporarily Queen-of-Sheba retired it is no concern of mine.

"Do you want to look at any other places?" Ethan asks. "I really like this one. It's peaceful. It'll only take me twenty minutes to get to work."

I nod. It is peaceful. And beautiful. I imagine myself reading on the balcony in the early afternoons, making dinner in the evening in the small kitchen while I watch the motion of the water. It seems ironic to me that I needed to come to Minnesota to finally have water views.

"I think I could live here," I say. "Yes. Let's try it."

Ethan opens the slider and steps inside, and I feel as though I am in a movie where, with that motion, everything starts.

Just before I follow him inside, a bird lands on the railing. I turn slowly to look at it. It is black, smudges of deep red on its wings.

I softly call Ethan back out, point, whisper, "What kind of bird is that?"

"It's a red-winged blackbird."

I laugh.

"No, it is."

"Oh," I say. "It seemed too obvious."

"Well," he says, "that happens."

21

Two months later, I am making bagels. I bought a book on bread, and I am trying what I believe to be the hardest thing. This is what happens when you have difficulty finding a job.

I thought I might enjoy not working. It happens not to be true. And unless I want a position manning a deep fryer, there is no work for me out here. The high point of my day thus far is that I have discovered sesame seeds in the bottle look just like sesame seeds on the bun.

After the badly formed bagels have been boiled and are in the oven, I lie on the sofa, close my eyes, think, What's so *bad* about this? You can listen to music, read a book, learn to sew—you can make a quilt! You get to walk for as long as you want every day; you see the animals that live in the woods, the little children who live in your neighborhood. You're living with Ethan, he comes back here every night, he sees you every day, he is sharing this pregnancy, isn't this what you dreamed of?

And then I answer myself. What's wrong with this is that I don't know what to do with myself. I haven't been able to make friends—no one is home during the day. The novelty of having time to write letters has worn off. I have called everyone, including the Berkenheimers, too often; there is not enough to say. I have paced in the living room at two in the afternoon for what I thought was an endless amount of time; then looked at my watch and found that it was two in the afternoon. I thought that there might be measurable joy in the billowing up of sheets you put on a bed that you share with someone you love. I forgot he needed to love you back in the same way.

I'm not really living with Ethan. He is living with his baby-to-be and its incubator, that's how it feels. When we were best friends I at least had some part of him that was only mine. Now I'm taking a backseat to my stomach, feeling, in some ways, more alone than ever. I lie beside him in bed at night, feeling warmth coming from his body but not touching him. It's torture, actually.

I don't know what I imagined. Did I think that the Midwestern climate would effect in him some deep change of heart and mind? That, free of a lifestyle that made certain demands on him, he would accept another possibility, enter into it fully?

Well, as it happens, yes. One night after we first moved in, remembering that he had called me his wife, I reached for him, gently rubbed his back. I felt him stiffen, and I stopped, pulled away, decided to wait for him to take the initiative. And waited. And waited. For what I know now will never come again. And yet I wait still. "Dear Patty," an advice columnist who lives in my head writes me daily, "You live with a *gay man.* Hellllooooo!" Ethan kisses my forehead, full of the only kind of love he can give, and my heart folds in on itself, dies.

I thought, too, that my pregnancy would be softly all-consuming, that I would be as in love with growing the baby as Ethan is. And for a time, I was. When Elaine visited shortly after we moved here, she walked into the bathroom and found me naked before the mirror, admiring myself. I blushed, reached for a towel, but she said, "No, let me see." We both looked at my rounded belly, my full breasts. "It's beautiful," she said softly.

I nodded. "You know, when I first started getting a belly I used to get up really slowly. I was afraid if I moved too fast, it would fall away. You know, disappear."

"No chance of that now," Elaine said.

"No," I said. "Not now." And we stared together again at my finally undeniably six-month-pregnant self.

Well, that was then; this is now. Let Elaine believe I am blissfully happy; let someone keep believing that. The truth is that I do not pay much attention to pictures showing how wonderfully developed my baby now is inside me, how talented, what with his thumb sucking, his somersaulting, his hearing. I pay attention to the fact that I need antacids for heartburn, and that I have suffered the supreme humiliation of asking my doctor if that was a *hemorrhoid* down there or what.

"Oh yes," he said, his voice rising up from between my legs. "Uh-huh, that's exactly what it is. Very common, don't worry." And he patted my knee, gave me a tight little smile.

"How was work?" I imagined his wife asking him at dinner that night, passing him the mashed potatoes. "Disgusting," I imagined him answering.

I dressed in anger after the examination that day, my teeth

clenched. And then, putting my hands to my belly, I wept, saying, "Sorry. Sorry."

The phone rings. "What are you doing?" Ethan asks.

I hate when he does this. Because I'm never doing anything, really. But "Making bagels," I answer, dutifully.

"You're kidding!"

"No."

"I didn't know you knew how to do that."

"Ethan? Let's go out to dinner tonight. And to a movie or something." Then on to Paris.

"Tomorrow, okay? I have to go out to dinner with a client tonight, that's why I'm calling."

"What client?"

"Bob Saunders is his name, I've never met him."

I am silent, twisting the phone cord around my wrist, murdering it. I recall when we were in the grocery store last Saturday, and Ethan passed a handsome man who stared at him and Ethan stared back. Just a little. But enough. The moment had the simultaneous brevity and interminability of an electric shock.

"Patty?"

"Forget it, Ethan. I'll just go alone to the movie."

"You can't wait one day?"

I stare out the window at the lake, blue-green today, just like yesterday, a sailboat off in the distance, free. "Fine," I say, and hang up. My voice is so flat. My self is so flat. Well, my *in*side self. I feel divorced from my own vitality, my own life spark. I feel as though I could run a hand down between my self and my self, as though some distance exists there between what I used to be and what I am, no bridge between them. I remember hearing women gaily say, "Oh, when you're pregnant, your mind just turns to *mush*!" I don't know what in the hell they were so happy about.

I open the oven door, stare in at my creation. "*You're* not bagels," I say. I throw them in the garbage, put Janis Joplin's "Ball and Chain" on the stereo. I turn it up high, then higher, then hear the neighbor pounding on the wall. I pound back, then turn the stereo down. There, I think. Okay? Okay?

"Now, I'm not going to kid you," the childbirth instructor tells us. "Labor is uncomfortable."

She pauses, waits. No one moves.

"But you'll get through it just fine. Some of you will have to use a little something"—she pauses, ever so slightly—"but *many* of you will need absolutely nothing at all." She beams.

"That won't be me, I'm just telling you," I say to Ethan.

"Shhhh!" He is nearly transfixed, watching the instructor pace before her blackboard, pointing to various disgusting illustrations. "Pay attention, Patty, we're going to need to remember this."

I don't know why he thinks so. I don't believe my time will ever come. I am not sure a baby is even in me. It's probably a tumor. Maybe it's gas. I have heard the rapid heartbeat, and I let Ethan be the one to be thrilled. I have rejected the earnestness of that rhythm. I refuse to believe the promise. I cannot engage.

When I see a newborn wrapped in a blanket and in my arms, maybe then we'll have something to talk about. I do not look at pregnancy books anymore; instead, I look at books with pictures of live babies. I see them staring amazed at the sight of light through their fingers; chewing busily on the leg of a doll, their silky eyebrows furrowed in baby concentration. I see them bending one small finger against their mother's breast, smiling with their whole bodies; I see them pushing Cheerios around on a high-chair tray. I look into their clear, wide eyes; I trace the lines of their hair with my finger. I ignore the Stages of Labor and focus instead on corduroy overalls, striped T-shirts, plastic butterflies trapped in clear balls that are held in the dimpled hands of tiny scientists. Until I have that for myself, until a real live baby is here, I am only enduring a state of body that makes tying shoes a near-Olympian feat. Ethan and Dr. Homer have had little chats about me, I know. I am a bit depressed, says Dr. Homer (who, by the way, has NO taste in clothes). Common thing in pregnancy, and in a move, too. When you combine the two, why . . .

Ethan and I both have a little crush on the father who sits on the floor beside us in childbirth class. I hear the gentle words of encouragement he offers his sweet-faced wife; and I see the difference between him and Ethan. Ethan may say many of the same things to me, but the source of those words, the impetus behind them—the meaning, ultimately—is achingly different. I know it with my head and my heart and my uterus and my lungs and the marrow in my bones. And I am tired of it. And so I am withdrawing from this pregnancy, which is not full of holiness and miracles. I quit. I just want a four-year-old who is my child, living with just me, thinking I am a yahoo hero and his dad is . . . okay.

"I want you ALL to practice your *BREATH*ing," the instructor says. "We're in tranSItion, now." She paces before us in her white coat, her pointer lightly slapping her leg like a riding crop. She has a very flat belly. "On three, all right? One . . . two . . . *three*!"

I want to kill her. I really might kill her.

That night, in bed, Ethan pulls me to him. "What *is* it?" he asks. "What's wrong?"

"Oh, Ethan, for God's sake, don't be so obtuse."

"Patty, I thought I made it clear, I can't . . . I don't—"

"I know!"

He pushes my hair back from the sides of my head, kisses the top of it. Big brother. "What can I do? What should I do?"

"I think you should move out for a while," I say. And cannot believe I have said it. Because it is, of course, the opposite of what I want. I want him to live with me *really,* to love me the way a man loves a woman when a man loves women. I am as hopelessly stubborn as the child who stands at the window crying for the moon to live in her toy box, to be brought out at will and held in her hands.

Ethan's arm loosens about me. I feel his chest rise as he takes in a breath. "You want me to move out? Are you serious?"

"Yes." I sit up, look at him. "It's not working at all, Ethan, the way we live."

He nods slowly.

"I hate it. I'm starting to hate you."

"Well. Jesus, Patty."

I shrug. "It's true."

"You know, Dr. Homer—"

"Oh, fuck him. I hate him. I can't believe Dr. Carlson even recommended him." Inside me, the baby moves, and, instinctively, I put my hand there. Ethan reaches out to feel too, and I say, "Don't."

"Patty. Should we just go back? Do you want to go home?"

"I don't know! I just want you to move out. I want . . . myself back. I don't know why you asked me to do this, Ethan. What did you think? What did you want?"

He sighs deeply. "I wanted . . . I guess I hoped I'd change, Patty. I know now it was a stupid idea. But I felt a terrible kind of desperation. I just couldn't . . . You remember when I was helping to take care of Bob Slater, the one that died right before we moved?"

"Of course. He's the one that told you the good thing about having AIDS was charging things and knowing he wouldn't have to pay for them. The one who was so good at *Jeopardy.*"

"Yeah. I told you all the charming things about Bob. His Marilyn Monroe wig. His Kewpie-doll collection. I didn't tell you he's the nineteenth person I've helped die. I didn't tell you about how it felt to drag him out of bed and put him on the commode and feel his head leaning into my stomach while he wept. I didn't tell you about how it feels to change sheets that are just . . . reeking, and then immediately change them again. I watched him lose his vision, he screamed the night it was finally gone, he just shook and screamed. Patty, do you know how many memorial services I've gone to? At first, I always felt so moved. Now it's like some horrible rou*tine* that just keeps going on and on and on. I've lost so many of my friends, Jesus, when I think of how many . . . I dream about them, once I dreamed there was a party and they were all there and I woke up sobbing, I missed them all so much. It got so that I was lying in bed at night, almost every night, thinking it's not fair, why don't I have it, I should have it, too. And then the phone would ring and it was the next new diagnosis. I just wanted *out* of that! At any cost. I was willing to try *any*thing to . . . just . . . you know, live some normal *life,* and it's true, I do want children. And I was just so tired of that phone and those apartments full of medical equipment and bottles of pills and the shades pulled all day, and then the dividing up of someone's stuff—here, you take his CDs, you get his Armanis, you take the fucking Weber grill! I'm a young man and all I was talking about was dying and dying and dying!"

He starts crying, silently, but I can feel the bed shake. "Ethan," I say, and I put my arms around him. "Ethan."

"You can't know," he says. "It was such a relief to just think about *life* for a change! I just wanted so much to have a piece of a happy life. I'm sorry. I know I've hurt you, and I swear, Patty, I never meant to."

"I know, Ethan."

"I do love you."

"I know that, too. You sleep, now, all right?"

"Patty? If you need me to go, I'll—"

"No. It's hard, Ethan, that's all. You just have to let me be crabby sometimes, it's hard to love you and not make love to you."

"I could try. We could." He kisses my forehead, my cheek, and I stop him.

"I think that might only be worse. We'll just keep what we have, all right?"

"Do let's keep it, though."

I nod, nod, nod.

• • •

A week later, we go to the doctor's office and hear that everything is proceeding nicely, that I should probably deliver close to my due date, in three weeks. We bring some groceries home and put them away and when we decide to go to a movie and get back in the car, it won't start. And because I am tired and vaguely sad I am awful and I yell at Ethan for not knowing anything about cars.

"I do know something," he says. "It's the battery. We need a new battery."

"Well, I'd like to know how we're going to get to a store to get a battery without a car! And what if I go into labor right now!"

He says nothing. He crosses the road and stands there hitch-hiking. Two hours later, a late model Mercedes pulls up in the driveway. I see Ethan emerge from the passenger side, carrying a battery and an armful of freesia. The driver, an older woman, toots the horn at him and waves when she leaves. Massachusetts license plates. I open the door, watch Ethan climb the steps up toward me.

"Who was that?" I ask.

"She picked me up hitchhiking," Ethan says. "Nan, her name was. I didn't have a *car,*" he reminds me.

I put the flowers in water, set them in the middle of the kitchen table, and burst into tears.

He crosses the room, holds me. "Tell me," he says. "Tell me what you want; I'll do it if I can."

"You can't do it."

"But I'll do anything else, Patty."

"Yeah. I know." I look around the living room, let out a shuddering sigh. "I want to go home, okay?"

"Okay."

"You want to come?"

"Yes."

"I think maybe I'll live alone again."

"I'm sorry."

"Yeah," I say. "I thought everything might change here, too."

He lets go of me, looks down into my face.

"Don't say anything," I say. "I know."

"I just wish you would be happy about the baby."

"I'll be happy about the baby when it gets here. If it gets here—it might not get here. I might be like this for the rest of my life."

"It will be here in less than a month, Patty. Think of that! We can leave in a week, all right? I'll give them a week's notice, and we'll drive back."

"Maybe the leaves will be starting to turn."

"Yes. Here, too."

"Not the same."

"You're right. Listen, let's go to the movie. I'll put the battery in."

I nod, feel relief filling my throat. When the phone rings, I answer it mindlessly.

"Honey?" my father says.

"What happened?" It is his voice that makes me say this, which is not his voice. I see Ethan step forward, his face full of questions. I hold up my hand. *Later.*

"Now, it's not an emergency," my father says.

"What happened?"

"Well, it's just that . . . your mother . . . She has Alzheimer's disease, Patty."

I laugh. "No, she doesn't."

"Well. Yes, she does."

"I . . . When did you find out?"

"A while ago. Now, we didn't want to tell you, but things have really—"

"What do you mean you didn't want to tell me?"

"Your mother was very firm on this point, Patty. She wanted you to get through this pregnancy without—"

"I'm coming home. Right now."

"Well, don't—"

"I'll be there as soon as I can."

"Listen to me. It's not an emergency. You be careful."

"I'll be careful. I want to come home. I was coming home anyway. I'm coming home."

"Oh, honey. Hey. Don't cry. We're all going to get through this."

I hang up the phone, turn to Ethan.

"Get in the car," he says. "You can tell me on the way."

I throw some things into a suitcase, say nothing while I'm packing except "I knew it." And realize that I did, too; of course I did.

22

My sisters and my brother are home, sitting at the dining-room table and having dinner when I walk in.

"*Look* at you!" my mother says, and embraces me. I am so sorry I left at all; my regret makes me dizzy.

"You just missed a couple of months," I say. And do not cry. And do not cry.

She squeezes me tighter, says quietly, "I'm all right. I'm all *right*."

I go around the table, hugging everyone, and then remember Ethan, who stands now in the corner of the room, unsure as to what he should do.

"Would you like to stay for dinner, Ethan?" my mother asks. She is like a Tupperware hostess: serenely surreal.

He looks at me. "I think . . . why don't I come back another time?"

I nod, grateful.

He smiles, waves a general good-bye, and is gone.

I sit at the table, take a bite off Johnny's plate while I'm waiting for my own. "It's good," I say. Turkey. Green beans. Stuffing. She's made it a million times, I know her recipe for everything. "So. We need to talk, huh?"

"Not tonight, Patty," my mother says. "Okay? We decided we'd have a nice dinner, all of us together, and talk in the morning."

"That's fine," I say. I look at my sister Donna, whose eyes are full of tears. "New 'do, huh?"

Her hand goes to the back of her neck. "I hate it. She used the *shaver.*"

"You've got to keep your eye on them every minute," I say. And then, to my sister Phyllis, "How are you?"

She nods, starts to speak, then just nods again.

It is the oddest dinner, the gentlest thing. Truly. It is so gentle. We might be underwater, the way everything is so wavy and muffled.

Later, after everyone has gone to bed, I lie awake on the sofa bed in my father's den. It feels so natural, so right, to have everyone back together under one roof again—no spouses, no children, just us. I remember the comforting clutter that used to be in this house: baseball gloves, schoolbooks, someone's jacket forever on some chair. The phone rang and rang and rang; voices shouted up the stairs, answers came ringing down. The upstairs bathroom mirror was continually fogged. I recall so many Christmases, all of us in our robes, and I smile, remembering the year Phyllis wanted to wear a lit Advent wreath and singed her hair, the year our dog ate the gift cheese and threw up all over the sofa while we were at midnight mass. I think of how loud dinners used to be, with competitive stories, laughter, occasional fights—often over who got the last of something. My mother laid out snacks for us every day after school; I wonder if anyone does that anymore. We got peanut-butter cookies, we got oranges slices in pretty arrangements; we got cocoa piled high with marshmallows.

I realize I am hungry. I hate when ordinary needs intrude on a melancholy reverie, but there you are, that's a body for you.

I put on my robe, head for the kitchen. I'll have a turkey sandwich, heavy mayo, what's the difference when you're as huge as I am. I turn on the light, see my father at the kitchen table. "Oh!" he says.

"Hey, Dad." I sit opposite him.

"Nice robe," he says. "Pretty."

"Ethan got it."

"That right?"

"Yeah, he outfitted me and the baby like you wouldn't believe."

"Well, that's nice."

"Dad?"

"Yeah."

"What are you doing down here, sitting in the dark?"

"Nothing. Can't see to do anything."

I smile, then say, "Could you . . . talk to me a little bit about things now? Just a little."

"Yeah, sure, honey." He leans back in his chair, rubs his hands together. "I'm glad you're home."

"Me, too."

A long pause, and then, "Well, we think this first started happening maybe six, eight months ago." He looks up at me and on his face is a terrible vulnerability, as though what he is about to reveal now is suddenly arbitrary, and it is up to me to make fact or fiction of it. For the first time in my life, I see the boy in him.

"Uh-huh," I say, gently. He has to finish. I need to know it all.

"She . . . well, you know, she had those mood changes. And she does get a little confused. It's just . . . starting to happen more often. Not all the time, though!"

"No."

"And, uh . . . Well, she started . . . She . . . " He pushes back away from the table. "Could you . . . ? I'll be right back. Okay?"

"Are you all right?"

"Oh, yeah. I'm fine. I'll be right back." He goes into the little downstairs bathroom, closes the door quietly.

I sit for a minute, then go to stand outside the bathroom door. Inside, I hear him quietly retching. I remember that his mother did this when his father died—she vomited over and over. She was lying on the sofa in a darkened living room, her yellow scrub bucket by her side, the afghan over her, though it was a hot summer day. She lay quietly, like a dead person herself, except to rise up now and then and hang over the bucket. I remember thinking, Well, that's good, that's a way to get the grief out. Now I understand the absurdity of that hopeful notion. I hear my father flush the toilet, turn on the tap. I think he may be looking at the image of himself in the mirror and seeing Miss Marilyn White, his pink-cheeked bride, twenty years old and saying *I do* with her mouth, with her eyes, with the slight slanting of her body toward his, the oblique line of love. She is brushing her auburn, then graying hair; smiling at him in her vanity mirror. She is scraping out a striped mixing bowl, patting down pincurls, opening her own mouth when she feeds their baby applesauce. She is turning up the radio and singing along with her favorite song, clapping her hands over her mouth when she sees the kitchen he remodeled for her, shielding her eyes against the setting sun last summer, when she came out into the backyard wearing her new sleeveless yellow dress and no shoes—earthily beautiful and plainly his. I'm sure that's what he's seeing. And seeing. And seeing. I pull my robe tighter around me, go back to the kitchen table, and wait for him.

In the morning, I go to the window and look out into the backyard. My mother is sitting in a lawn chair, her head thrown back, letting the sun fall on her face. It must be chilly; she has a sweater clutched around her. I look at my watch: 7:40.

I go into my parents' room. Empty, the bed neatly made, framed pictures on the dresser speckled by dust that nearly glitters in the strong morning light. I get a pair of my father's warmest socks, put his robe and slippers on, join my mother in the back-yard.

"Say, there's an attractive outfit," she says.

"It's warm," I say. And then, "It's *cold*!"

"Well, it's early."

"Where's Dad?"

"He went to the bakery. You want some coffee?"

"No thanks, Mom. I can't—"

"Oh! Yes, I remember. I remember that."

"Okay."

"You look wonderful, honey."

"I hate being pregnant."

She laughs.

"I do! I thought it would be so wonderful but it's just a pain in the ass."

"Don't use that language in front of me."

"Sorry. But it is."

"Well," she says. "Just *wait*."

I look at her. "What do you mean?"

"Pain in the ass?" she says. "You want to know about pain in the ass?" She laughs again. Well. *She's* certainly in a good mood.

"It's not pain in the ass you have when you deliver," I say, looking down.

"I hated being pregnant, too," my mother says, suddenly.

I look up. "You *did*?"

"Yes. Does that surprise you?"

"Well . . . *yes*. You never said anything."

"Wasn't worth it. I said it to your father, he knew. But there was no reason to tell all of you. Anyway, I loved children, I just hated the pregnancies."

"God!" I say. "God!"

"Are we praying, Patty?"

"Ma. I just . . . I wish I'd known that. It would have made me feel so much less guilty."

"Oh, don't feel guilty." Her voice is bitter now. "It's such a waste of time." She looks around the yard, at the fading garden, at the trees just starting to turn. Together, we listen to the staccato message of a woodpecker, and together we smile at it.

"What else?" I say.

"What?"

"What else can you tell me about pregnancy that might be useful? Not that I have much more time left. If there's a God in heaven."

"Oh, I don't know. Relax."

Something occurs to me. I need her. I swallow, look away.

"What?" she says.

"Nothing. I'm just thinking."

"Thinking what? Patty?"

"Just . . . I need you. You know?"

"Well. I'm here."

"I know, but I need you to keep telling me things."

"Oh, I'll always tell you things. I live in you."

A car door slams, then a house door. Then we hear my father yelling, "Marilyn? *Mar*ilyn?"

"We're out here!" she yells back. Then, to me, quietly, "For heaven's sake. He's never going to make it."

23

Ethan and I are sitting in the parking lot of the Mary C. Conway Center for Alzheimer's. It is a handsome building, a brick exterior, evergreen-colored trim, a well-kept lawn. We have an appointment to talk to the director in fifteen minutes.

The afternoon after I came home, my mother napped while the rest of us sat in the living room and talked about whether we would ever have to—or be able to—institutionalize her. "She's not *that* bad!" I said, and Johnny said, "She's had a couple of good days in a row. But we have to face the fact that she's getting worse. Last week she was trying to use a fork to drink milk. And she left her slippers on the stove. And—"

"All right," I said. "But she doesn't have to be put somewhere! I'll help take care of her. And Dad will. There are home health aides you can hire. And . . . day care. For adults." At this, Phyllis and I both began crying, and my father didn't look far from it. We all stopped talking when my mother suddenly appeared, saying, "Enough. I won't have my family falling apart before I do." She sat down in a chair beside my father, smoothed her skirt. "Now. What's for dinner?" she asked.

"You want to go in now?" Ethan asks.

"No."

"You want to just wait here till it's time?"

"No."

"Patty."

"Oh, all right, let's go in."

We go through a set of double glass doors and encounter an older man dressed in a three-piece suit, a hat on his head, a cane in hand. "I wonder if you could help me," he says to Ethan.

"Yes?"

The man takes Ethan's hand, leans in close to him. "Well, but I wonder if you could *help* me."

"I'll try."

"Where's my room?"

"Oh. Sorry, I don't know."

"I just moved here," the man says. "Used to be in the armed forces."

"Uh-huh."

"Damned if I know where my room is!"

"Well, let's ask," I say. "There's a nurse; let's ask her."

Together we approach the nurse, who is standing in the hall before a medication cart. She looks up and smiles. "Hi, Henry. Are you giving these people a tour?"

"Well, I'm a little lost," Henry says. "I just moved here."

"No, hon, you've been here for two years. Okay?"

"Oh yes," Henry says, and takes her outstretched hand, shuffles along beside her.

"Did you need some help?" the nurse asks us, over her shoulder.

"Yes," Ethan says, at the same time that I say, "No thank you."

I walk out quickly, Ethan close behind me. Outside, he says, "What, you don't want to stay?"

"No."

"Okay. But let me just go back in and cancel the appointment."

"I'll be in the car."

I make my way on feet that have gone numb, then sit and stare out the windshield.

When Ethan returns, he says, "She said if you change your mind, come back any time."

I nod, stare out at the trees. The colors must be breathtaking to anyone who can really see them.

"It wasn't so bad there, Patty."

I say nothing.

"I mean, it was . . . clean. And—"

"No, Ethan."

"All right."

He starts the car, drives slowly out of the lot. I sit quietly, remembering a time when my parents went out and I was babysitting for the younger ones, and we decided to snoop around. It had been a long time since we'd done it. We got very organized, divided up the house. I got my parents' room, and I checked the closet, the bureau, under the bed. There was nothing. Then I looked in my mother's night-table drawer, which never yielded anything but cough drops and Kleenex and paperback novels and her pink rosary, but we had vowed to be thorough. This time, in addition to the usual, I found a half-eaten Heath bar, wrapped up with a rubber band. I was a little angry about this; I loved Heath bars, and she had never offered one to me. I also found a list with menu ideas for a week—under Tuesday was "San Francisco pear salad??" I guess she decided against it, since I never remember having it. She'd also listed stuffed peppers for another night; and for Friday, she'd planned "Italian spaghetti." I still remember that list as plainly as if I were holding it in my hand right now. Also in the drawer was a little pile of photos, pictures of hairdos cut out from magazines, models with hair approximately the length of my mother's, in greatly varying styles. This surprised me. I had no idea my mother cared about her hair. I was fifteen and completely self-obsessed; the notion that my mother, too, worried about hairstyles irritated me. And yet I felt a kind of tenderness toward her that made me not share any of her drawer's contents with anyone else. I said I'd not found anything interesting at all. I didn't want to betray her.

The next week, coincidentally, I'd found another surprise: a pair of ballet slippers in a cupboard in the laundry room. This room was not one that we ever looked in during our snoop sessions. But I'd needed bleach for a science experiment and when I pulled it out from the cupboard, I saw a brown paper bag pushed toward the back, and inside were pink toe shoes. They were beautiful, with wide pink ribbons wrapped neatly around them. The shoes were old, but hardly used; the soles were nearly perfect. I put them back. Not long afterward, I asked my mother about them, and she said, "Oh, you found those, huh? Yes, I bought them for myself a few years ago. I saw them in the window of a store that sold dancewear one time when your father and I went to New York. And I went in and just . . . bought them."

"But why?" I asked.

"Why?" She smiled, consulted her hands for an answer I might understand. "To dance, I guess."

"When do you ever dance?"

"Oh," she said, "sometimes when you are all in school. I just put them on and . . . Well, I don't really *dance.* I try, I guess, but mostly I just walk around a little, stand on my toes, do a little pirouette. . . ."

"How *come?*" I was mortified. I didn't want her to do it anymore.

She laughed. "I don't know." And then she went off to answer the phone and we never talked about it again.

Now I see my mother pulling those ballet shoes out of the paper bag, sitting on the red vinyl step stool next to the dryer, raising her housedress up over her knees. I see her sliding off her loafers, winding beautiful pink ribbons around her forty-year-old ankles, then standing, just for one brief moment, *sur la pointe,* to the applause of clinking buttons and zippers in the dryer. I didn't know if she ever came out of the laundry room to dance. And now I'm afraid to ask her, for fear she will say, "What ballet slippers?"

I am so selfish. Never mind all that my mother faces. I am so afraid of what *I* will lose when she forgets.

"You want to eat something?" Ethan asks now.

"Yes," I say. And then, I say, "Oh!"

"What?" he says. "What'd you forget?"

"Nothing," I say. "I think . . . I'm in labor." The word sounds so stupid. Forced, as in when you learn a new vocabulary word and then feel compelled to use it the next day.

"Not yet," Ethan says. "It's not time yet."

I look over at him, and he looks back at me.

"You want to tell the baby that?" I say. And then, "You want to take me to the hospital?"

"Should we pull over?" he says. "Should we call an ambulance?"

"No. It's a first labor. This will take about six thousand hours. You remember what they said about first labors, right?"

"I don't remember anything." He signals right, turns left. "How bad does it hurt?"

I put my hand to my belly, as though this will help me tell better. And in a way, it does: I can feel a tightening when the pain comes. "It's pretty much like not-so-bad menstrual cramps," I say. "On . . . you know, the second day."

"Ah," Ethan says. "Thank you. That clears it right up."

An hour later, I am back at home, sitting in my living room with Elaine. Ethan and Mark have gone out to pick up some Chinese food from the expensive new restaurant we've all been dying to try. Apparently we're going to celebrate my idiocy.

"Dr. Carlson was really nice," I say. "But it was so embarrassing! They put me in a room right away, took me before all the broken arms and *bleeding* people, and then it was *noth*ing!"

"Well, how are you supposed to know?" Elaine asks.

"I *am* supposed to know! Between Ethan and me, we've read about fifty-five books; we took that stupid class . . . "

"But you haven't been through it before."

"No."

"I'm so glad you're back here. I want to see when it really happens."

"Great."

"No," she says, "it'll be fun."

I look at her. "Why don't you just get pregnant? Then you can see for yourself?"

"Actually—"

"Are you serious?"

"Six weeks."

"Elaine!"

She shrugs. "Are you glad?"

"Well . . . yeah! Aren't you?"

"Well . . . Did you ever get that black line down your belly?"

"No."

"Okay. Then I'm glad."

I hug her, then say, "We are very superficial people."

"I suppose." She leans back, stretches, then says, "How's your mom?"

Ah. Yes. That. "I don't know. Diagnosed, you know—I guess that's the difference. Now that it has that name, it's so much scarier. She's actually handling it the best of all of us. My father is a wreck."

"Yeah. He would be. I never saw a man so much in love for such a long time. I always think of that story he told us about jumping off the ship when he was in the navy—remember, to get the letter your mother had sent that blew out of his hands?"

"Yeah. And you know what my mother told me the other day? When they were first married, she wanted lilacs in their backyard. They couldn't afford to buy any bushes, so my father went into some rich people's neighborhood and tried to steal some. He got arrested!"

"Wow! Really? He has a record? Lilac thief?"

"I guess. He might have gotten away with it if he'd only taken one, but he was trying to stuff five or six of them into the back of his car."

The door opens and the smell of Chinese food wafts in. "Ummmmm," I say. And then, "Ohhhh!"

Three pairs of eyes turn to look at me.

"This is not like menstrual cramps," I say.

"Oh, Jesus," Ethan says, and Elaine asks excitedly, "Is this real? Is this the real one?"

I sit down. Someone has lassoed my uterus and is trying to drag it out of my body.

"This is real," Ethan says. And then, to Elaine, "Want to come this time?"

"Call my mother," I say. And walk out to Ethan's car with my mouth wide open, which I think is not how I am supposed to be breathing.

"Bring my bag!" I yell, over my shoulder.

"I've got it!" Ethan says, running up quickly behind me.

"Help," I say quietly, as he fastens his seat belt.

"What?" Ethan starts the engine. He is a little wild-eyed.

"Oh, God," I say. "Look what we did."

He takes my hands. "You're going to do just fine. I'm going to be right with you, okay?"

I nod, then say, *"Ow!"*

"Here we go. We're going now." Ethan puts the car into gear, and we are off.

Right behind us is Mark's car. I see Elaine crying and waving at me. I wave back, smile weakly, face front again. "What time is it?" I ask Ethan. My watch says 7:22 but I want to be sure.

"Seven twenty-two."

"All right then," I say. And then, "Wait. Wait. It doesn't hurt now."

"Okay, so let's time them, starting with the next one. That's what we're supposed to do. Write it down—there's pen and paper in the glove compartment."

"No, I'm telling you it went away. It doesn't hurt! At *all.*"

Ethan looks at me, a bit murderously.

"Go back home," I say. "We'll eat. We're all starving."

"Go back home?"

"Yes."

"Patty . . ."

"It's just another false alarm," I say. "Although—" I swallow, lean my head back against the seat, close my eyes. "Whoa."

"That's it!" Ethan says. "We're going. And I'm timing this."

"Well," I say weakly. "Good. That'll show it who's boss."

Ten hours later, Ethan sits on one side of me, my mother on the other. Mark and Elaine went home hours ago. My father got kicked off the maternity unit forty-five minutes after we arrived for trying to boss the nurses around. He ferried food up and down for everyone but me, which is grossly unfair since I'm the one who's doing all the work. I don't see what one taco would hurt.

We are in the birthing room, which has cheerful yellow curtains on a window framing a view of heating ducts. There is a pastel-colored quilt on the wall opposite me that I liked very much when I arrived and would now like to rip apart with my teeth.

My mother has been telling me over and over that I'm doing

fine. Now, having just learned that the amazing increase in the level of pain means I'm "progressing nicely," she tries to distract me from my agony by telling me what she saw on the way to the hospital. "We went past the Richmond place, you know that beautiful estate for sale over by the lighthouse?"

"Two point four mil." I grit my teeth, grunt loudly, then say, "Excuse me."

"That's fine, honey, you make all the noise you need. Scream if you want to, you just go right ahead."

"I'm not screaming!"

"Well, I didn't say you *were,* I just said to *do* it if you want to!"

"I *don't* want to!"

A nurse pops her head in the door. "Doing okay? Are you sure you don't want anything for pain?"

"*No!!* Thank you."

"No?" my mother asks. "Honey?"

"No!" I say. "I don't . . . it might hurt the baby."

"It doesn't hurt the baby. They wouldn't give it to you if it would hurt the baby!"

"Oh, please. Remember thalidomide? DES?"

"Well—"

"I'm not—*Ow!!*"

"It could help, honey."

"Oh, God, this is a big one, now."

"Okay. Concentrate," Ethan says, from the other side of me. "Big cleansing breath."

"Mom," I say.

"Yes?"

"Would you just . . . talk?"

"Okay," she says. "All right. So . . . the Richmond estate. It is such a lovely place, and the grounds! They have a big wrought-iron gate, you remember, and it was open partway and it just looked like the loveliest thing to me, you know? That open gate? It seemed so full of promise, I always feel that way about open gates, that they have this promise. Of course, it's a very fragile promise. We don't know, you know. We don't know."

"Mom?" I say. She looks close to crying.

"I'm awfully tired, honey. I'm afraid I'm going to have to leave this to you and Ethan. All right?"

I nod. "Yes. I'm sorry. I should have sent you home a long time ago. Thank you."

She stands, smiles at Ethan. "You'll call right away, right?"

"Of course."

"Ethan," I say.

"Yes?"

"Don't you leave."

"I'm not leaving, Patty."

"And where is Robert?" my mother asks.

"He's down in the main lobby," Ethan says. "You take the elevator right next door, he's right down there."

"To the lobby, then," she says.

"Yes."

She comes back to me, kisses my forehead. "You're fine. You'll do just fine. You have that baby, and then you call your mother."

"Okay." I watch her go out the door, then tell Ethan, "Go with her."

"You're sure?"

"Yes, but don't make her feel—"

"I won't. I'll be right back."

While Ethan is gone, Dr. Carlson comes, asks if he can check me. "Can you wait?" I ask. "I'm having a contraction."

"Sure." He takes my hand. "You're doing very well."

"Uh-huh." I am dying.

"I think you're awfully close. Where's Ethan?"

"Took. My mother. Downstairs."

"Let me check you, Patty."

"Still hurts."

"Yes, but let me check."

I turn onto my back. He is so amazingly cruel. I focus on the ceiling, then squeeze my eyes shut. And then hear a long, low growl I recognize vaguely as being myself.

"Oh, yes, uh-huh," Dr. Carlson says, at the same time Ethan walks back in.

"What is it?" Ethan asks.

"She's ready." Dr. Carlson goes to the door, leans out into the hall. "Nancy? Let's get her into a delivery room. She's going to go." He smiles at me. "We're going to get that baby to you now, Patty. I'm just going to change into clean scrubs."

Ethan, who is already in scrubs, sits in the chair my mother vacated, takes my hand. "This is it!"

"Ethan."

"Yes?"

"Come here."

He hesitates, pulls his chair closer, leans in toward me. "Yes?"

I take a handful of his shirt, pull him closer still. Then I whisper, "You have to take me home now. Okay? Don't tell them. Just take me home, right now. We'll come back for my things later."

He is silent for a moment. Then, "Patty?" he says. "You're having a baby."

"No," I say. "I'm not. And I want to go home, I really don't feel well."

"Okay, listen to me. You're dilated almost all the way and you're 100 percent effaced. Okay? You're going to have the baby now. We're not going anywhere but the delivery room."

"Ethan."

"Yes?"

"You are so letting me down."

"Oh, Patty." He kisses my hand.

"I want to go home."

"And you will. But first we're just going to do this one little thing, okay?"

I shudder hugely, grit my teeth, push down hard in a way that seems completely independent of me.

"See?" he says, quietly, apologetically.

I nod.

Behind him, the doctor and two nurses appear. "Okay, Ethan," one of the nurses says, "if you step back, we'll get her on the cart."

"Just a minute," Ethan says. And then, softly, to me, "I love you." I start crying, but I'm very happy.

"I'm right here," Ethan says. "I'm going to stay right beside you. Okay? We're going to the delivery room now, and I'm going to stay right here beside you."

I am moved onto the cart and brought into the delivery room, where it is so bright and cold.

"I'm freezing," I say, my teeth chattering. My legs are quivering. I see the white socks on my feet and I feel sorry for them.

A huge mirror is positioned above me.

"Can you see?" Dr. Carlson asks, from behind his mask.

"Yes. Yes." No.

"Okay, Patty, I want you to *push* now."

"I don't think so."

"Push!" he says.

"NO!"

Ethan leans down, his eyes to mine. "Everything is fine. You're just fine. But we were wondering . . . can you push a little?"

I push. But not a little, and not because he tells me to. I push because that is all there is in the world, and I push like what I mean to do is turn myself inside out. After a while I feel some bony softness slide down, then slip out of me. "Oops," I say, and then hear a cry. I look up into the mirror, see myself, my head on a pillow with a blue paper pillowcase. Down by my feet are some medical hands, and I see part of a live baby: a bent arm, fingers clenched into a fist. It is wrapped quickly into a blanket by the nurse.

"I think I'll let Ethan say what sex it is," Dr. Carlson says. Ethan lets go of my hand, walks to the end of the table, looks into the blanket. There is a moment of quiet, a year of quiet, and then he speaks. It is so soft, but I hear him say, "Hello, Marilyn." Then, with a tenderness I would not have thought possible in earthbound humans, he gives her to me. Her wet head is cupped; her quivering chest is calmed. What have my hands been doing all my life before this? I see now that they too have just been born. I unwrap the blanket, stop breathing.

24

" 'Marilyn' is a very good name," Muriel Berkenheimer says. She is standing beside me, looking through the nursery window at my daughter, sleeping deeply before us. "I'm glad you settled on that one."

"I used to have a girlfriend named Marilyn," Artie says.

"You say that about every girl's name you ever hear," Muriel says. Then, to me, "He does. Every name, it's 'I had a girlfriend with that name.' "

Artie shrugs. "I had a lot of girlfriends, Muriel." He pokes at her a little with his elbow. "Jealous?"

"That's it, I'm jealous."

I'm so happy to hear them carrying on in the old way. Artie looks good; he's doing far better than he was told he would. "I decided, what do they know?" he said, when we visited in my room. And Muriel said, "It's true. He was lying around one day, miserable—well, let's face it, we were both miserable, and he says to me, 'Oh the hell with it, Muriel, let's go get some tomato plants and put them in.' So we did. Next day he feels better, day after that, better still."

"Big Boys," Artie said.

"Pardon me?" I asked.

"Big Boy tomatoes, you can't go wrong with them."

"Anyway," Muriel said, "Dr. Singer says he can't believe Artie. But here he is. He's doing just fine."

"Well, for the time being," Artie said.

"He's doing fine," Muriel said. "And if you're going back to work anytime soon, we'd like to take a look at a few places. You could bring the baby, babies love me."

Now, tapping on the glass softly, Muriel says, "Good-bye, Marilyn." As though in response, the baby's lips move into an O shape, then relax.

"I told you, they love me," Muriel says. Then, lower, "I've always had big breasts, maybe that's it."

"Oy," Artie says. "Let's go."

I watch them walk away, then head back to my room. I've got to get my things together; I'm going home today. Ethan will pick me up in an hour. We'll have dinner at my parents' house, and then I'll go back to my apartment and start this new life.

When I am packed, I bring Marilyn's isolette into my room, watch her sleep. I think about a story I heard on the radio one night, about how a man with Alzheimer's disease created a beautiful rock garden, worked hard on it all his adult life. A short time after he developed the disease, he forgot that he was responsible for his own creation; he thought his sons had done it. Each day, he would walk out into it saying, "This is nice. They did a good job." Last night, I told Ethan about the story, and I was crying and saying, "Oh, God, isn't it terrible?"

He got very quiet and then he said, "You know, Patty, I haven't told you this because I wasn't sure how you'd take it. But I want to tell you now. I had an uncle who had Alzheimer's, and I used to visit him and my aunt a lot when I was around fifteen or so. I remember the room he was in before he died—they'd converted the dining room into a sickroom, and it was so bright in there, and so big. There were supplies stacked up all over the place, so neatly, and also things like seashells here and there, small bouquets. . . . I always had this funny feeling of it being such a pleasant place, but a kind of hell, too. At that point, Uncle Jim couldn't even talk, and he had this kind of masklike face."

I began crying harder and Ethan said, "No. Wait. Wait."

I wiped my eyes, lay back in the bed, took in a shuddering breath. "Okay. What."

"Well, the thing was . . . I was there one day and my Aunt Beck was talking about him, and about things they used to do together. And then she took one of Uncle Jim's hands and held it and looked at him; and she said, 'We had a love, didn't we, Jim?' and he looked up at her and . . . *smiled,* you know, he smiled, and I knew it was hard for him and I knew it was so rare. And I remember looking away from that, it seemed too much to see, the . . . brightness of that kind of love. I think it was such a testimonial, Patty, that's what I want to say to you. It's not something I'd wish on anyone, that kind of trial. But I think if anyone can *endure* this, with grace, and with spirit, and with a kind of gentleness, it's your parents. These kinds of things, whether it's Alzheimer's or AIDS, they're awful; but they're also the way that we can show our own greatness to each other." He shrugs, sighs.

"It seems pretty rare that we ever get to choose what will prove our love, really."

They wheeled Marilyn in then, red-faced and hungry, and I put her to my talented breast, soothed her.

Then I looked up at Ethan. "Then the way you see it, it's like the guy who did that rock garden gets to . . . receive it, again and again. To see it new, every day."

"He does."

"Well, that may be wonderful for him, in a way. But think how his wife's heart is broken every time he shows her how he doesn't even remember doing it."

"Maybe broken. Maybe strengthened. Maybe even with her pain, she is glad. About what he still has. And about what she can give him—is willing to."

I stared at him, blank-eyed.

"I know, I'm blathering on and on," he said.

"No," I said. "You make me feel much better." And I began sobbing, catching the tears so they wouldn't fall on Marilyn's head.

Now I sit imagining that my mother may do well for a long time, just like Artie. Or she may progress rapidly to a dementia that makes her surprised to see me with a baby every time I come over. In which case, will she not herself be a happy recipient, over and over? And is this not infinitely preferable to losing her all at once, say, to a heart attack? I don't know, but I think so.

My phone rings, and when I answer it, I hear Ethan say, "I'll be there early; is that okay?"

He will walk down the hall to my room, and the nurses will say, "Come look, that's the one." They think he's so handsome and they're right. They think I'm so lucky, and they're right about that, too. The man I love is gay, but he loves me back. I don't get to have the partnership I dreamed of for raising a baby, but I get to have a baby. Still Ms. Runner-up, I guess. It's true that there is some pain in coming close to something, and then not quite making it. There is also a lot of hard joy.

I look at my watch, lean down into Marilyn's isolette. She has awakened and now lies quietly, waiting for whatever might come. I open my purse and take out a picture, hold it above her, watch her seem to focus on one of the figures. "That's your daddy," I say. "He's coming to get us right now."

I start to put the picture away, then stop, look at it again. It is a picture of Ethan and me, the only one I had for a long time, and one I'd forgotten about until recently. It was taken in my apartment, not long after he told me he was gay. He'd been over for dinner with Elaine and me, and he was getting ready to leave. He and I were standing at opposite sides of a doorway, leaning against the jambs, our arms crossed. And then, I remember this, I reached out toward Ethan at exactly the same time that he leaned in toward me. That's when Elaine took the picture. I am smiling, my face lifted toward his and full of leftover hope. You can only see part of Ethan's face, but I remember exactly what his expression was: sorrow and love, an equal mix. I'm not sure about all we might have intended, moving toward each other that way, but there we are, met in the middle, me and Ethan, for a kind of eternity.

I put the picture back in my purse. Then I kiss Marilyn's cheek, and let my finger slide into her open hand, watch her hand close and hold on tight. I think I've always known that she'd be the one to guide me.

Epilogue

In three weeks Marilyn will be nine months old. I finally live in a small house by the ocean, which I bought with the earnings of a pretty spectacular sale I made. Marilyn's room, where I rock her now, is painted a butter yellow; and her curtains feature happy ducks, blue ribbons tied lazily around their necks. It's a warm summer day, and both of us have our eyes closed as we move back and forth, listening to the familiar creak of the chair.

I am thinking about my mother, about how this morning when I went over to visit she was out sitting on the back steps, wearing only her slip. My father had been in the bathroom, and he came flying out, red-faced and distressed, at the same time that I found her outside like that. We stood before her, unsure as to exactly what to say—we are still unsure, at such moments, though what usually works best is to say nothing, to simply move on to the next moment. But this time she spoke first. She looked up at us, smiled radiantly, and said, "Oh, well, then, this is wrong, isn't it?"

"Honey . . ." my father said.

She got up and straightened the back of her slip, then said to me, “And who is this beautiful child?”

“It’s Marilyn,” I told her. “Your granddaughter.”

“Of course it is,” my mother said, and reached out to take the baby. Marilyn leaned into my mother’s shoulder, put her thumb in her mouth, reached up for a piece of my mother’s hair. My mother looked at me then, and in her eyes was a piece of her old, confident self, the woman who could quiet any crying baby, the woman who, when it came to children, always knew the right thing to do. She was a builder of card houses extraordinaire, a constant tender of small wounds to the knee and grievous ones to the heart. She carried Marilyn inside, cooing to her, and Marilyn took her thumb out of her mouth to coo back.

My father looked at me. “I know,” he said. “I’m going to get some help. Someone’s coming today for an interview.”

“Okay.”

“I just want to keep her here. For . . . you know, as long as I can.”

“I know.”

He stared into the kitchen through the screen door. We could both see the dim outline of my mother, sitting at the kitchen table. She was singing to Marilyn; I thought I remembered the melody.

My father put his arm around me, squeezed. “I have to say she looks pretty damn good in a slip, though, don’t you think?”

I smiled. “Yeah.”

“When you look that good in a slip, why not wear it outside, huh?”

“Right.”

“Am I right?”

"Absolutely."

He kissed my forehead, told me quietly, "What keeps her going now, honey, is just the living itself. You know? Just the living itself."

"Well," I said, "I guess that's true for all of us. I mean, I would hope that it would be."

My grandmother, my mother's mother, had a certain platter she prized. She'd bought it at a department store—put it on layaway and made monthly payments of a dollar—thinking that if she ever got married, she'd display it in her china cabinet, bring it out on certain holidays. It got broken one Easter by my sister Phyllis, who had volunteered to carry it into the kitchen to be washed. There was a terrible moment of silence when it happened, and then my grandmother, who had her priorities straight, came and put her arm around Phyllis and said, "Now don't you feel bad. We're going to fix this, you and I, and when it is fixed, it will be even better than it was before." Not strictly true, actually, and we all knew it, especially Phyllis. But it was true enough, and the platter did get glued together and continued to be used year after year. It may not have been better than it was before in the most literal sense, but it gained a kind of dignity and worth from the way it was loved despite itself. Because of itself, actually.

I kiss the top of Marilyn's head, relish the silky feel of her hair, the sweet smell of her baby head. She has fallen asleep, but I continue to hold her anyway. Outside, the sky is a pale blue, the holy color of a fresco. I look up into it, rock and stare, remembering a whimsical belief I'd once enjoyed. I imagined I'd had a choice about whether or not to be born, that I was a perfectly happy angel in heaven and then my turn for The Conversation came up and God and I sat with crossed legs in his office full of clouds and He said, "So? You want to go?"

I said, "I don't know. What's involved?"

"Well," He said, "you'd go to Earth."

"Earth," I said.

"Yes," He said, "Earth. It's quite beautiful there. And of course you'd be living with human beings."

"What's 'human beings'?" I asked, and He sighed deeply, but He smiled, sighing, and there was so much tenderness there you knew His love far outweighed His regret.

"Human beings," He said. "They are the ones with the most important job. They are supposed to make what they want out of what they are given."

"Do they do it?" I asked, and He said, "Sometimes not. But sometimes so."

"Well," I said. "I'll go. I want to see."

I can't remember when I stopped entertaining this notion. Maybe I never did, really.

I put Marilyn down in her crib, pull her blanket up to her small ear, which has been reddened by our closeness. I pull down her shades, tiptoe out of her room. I need to start dinner; Elaine, Mark, Ethan, and his lover, Louis, will be over later. I think Ethan has found his someone; they're very happy together. And I know, I know, I know; but I really believe that what I have is enough, at least for now. Perhaps later I will find a someone, too. For now there is the creak of the rocker, the luscious fact of my sleeping daughter. There is the sound of the rushing waves, the sight of the ocean from nearly all the windows—I watch the water sparkle in the morning when I wash the breakfast dishes, and I see it moving under the stars every night before I sleep. I have friends and family whom I love in a town I love living in; I have wild roses climbing up the side of a house that belongs to me. The blossoms are a deep pink color, beautiful beside each other. Or by themselves.

About the Author

ELIZABETH BERG'S first novel, *Durable Goods*, was called a "gem" by Richard Bausch. *Talk Before Sleep* was a 1996 Abby Honor Book and a *New York Times* bestseller. *Range of Motion, The Pull of the Moon*, and *Joy School* were all critically acclaimed bestsellers. In 1996, Ms. Berg won the New England Booksellers Award for body of work. She lives with her dog, Toby, in Massachusetts, where she writes, cooks, quilts, and gardens, all with equal passion.

About the Type

This book was set in Perpetua, a typeface designed by the English artist Eric Gill, and cut by The Monotype Corporation between 1928 and 1930. Perpetua is a contemporary face of original design, without any direct historical antecedents. The shapes of the roman letters are derived from the techniques of stonecutting. The larger display sizes are extremely elegant and form a most distinguished series of inscriptional letters.